THE**MOTOR**NOVELS

Checkered Flag Cheater
Super Stock Rookie
Saturday Night Dirt

CHECKERED FLAG CHEATER

WILL WEAVER

Checkered Flag Cheater

FARRAR STRAUS GIROUX

New York

www.fsgteen.com

Library of Congress Cataloging-in-Publication Data
Weaver, Will.
    Checkered flag cheater / Will Weaver.— 1st ed.
        p.   cm. — (Motor novels)
    Summary: Trace Bonham, a teenaged professional stock car racer,
blows away the competition wherever he races, but with every victory
Trace is increasingly aware that his winning is due to more than just
his driving skills.
    ISBN: 978-0-374-35062-8
    [1. Stock car racing—Fiction.   2. Automobile racing—Fiction.
3. Cheating—Fiction.   4. Middle West—Fiction.]   I. Title.

PZ7.W3623Ch 2010
[Fic]—dc22
                                                    2009013600

Frontispiece: Photograph © Dennis Peterson

SPECIAL THANKS

to Skyler Smith, driver for Team Weaver Racing. We couldn't do it without you. Thanks also to Tom Jensen for his book *Cheating*, about the pursuit of speed in NASCAR, and to Lin Johnson for his tech tips.

CHECKERED FLAG CHEATER

1

Trace Bonham poked the Seek button. Radio stations were hard to find late at night in the eastern tip of Iowa— or maybe it was the car radio. This vehicle, bought for cash in Indiana, was an American tin can. The right front tire had a high-speed shimmy that vibrated his teeth, and the yellow headlight beams were like two flashlights with old batteries. However, all it had to do was get him home to Minnesota, then down to South Dakota to catch up with Team Blu. Driving this car at night was like driving his Team Blu Super Stock—keep the pedal down and hope that nothing happened just ahead . . .

"Don't be afraid of big dust or smoke in front of you," Harlan said. Harlan was Team Blu's crew chief. "In fact, it's best to drive straight into it, because whatever happened—whoever spun out or wrecked—ain't there anymore."

"Yeah, yeah," Trace muttered as he pulled on his helmet. Team Blu was ready for the twenty-lap feature—another high-banked short track where the circling stock cars spun up dust like a tornado stuck in neutral. Another state, another speedway, another exhibition race for Team Blu.

"Find yourself a middle line and stay in it," Harlan continued. "There's gonna be a lot of spinouts, and spinouts don't stay in the middle of the track, either—they end up over the fence or into the infield."

"You want to drive this thing?" Trace shot back.

"Are you kidding?" Harlan said. "It's way too dangerous —especially in a dust bowl like this track." His son, Jimmy Joe, the setup man on Team Blu, cackled with laughter. Even Smoky, their engine builder, croaked out a laugh.

Trace flipped down his visor and fired the engine. He spun the tires—and left a gift of fresh dust for Team Blu— as he headed down pit row. The pits were choked with haze, a combination of dust and poor lighting, and he made sure not to run into anybody. Then it was up the ramp and down onto the track.

Whether the track surface was dry, slick dust or tacky gumbo, there was nothing quite like merging with the rumbling parade of twenty other brightly lettered stock cars. He drew near his starting slot—last row, inside—but didn't take it immediately. Falling into line right away meant looking overeager. Like a rookie. Technically, Trace was a Super Stock rookie this year, but he had raced enough to know the mental game.

He scrubbed the tires—a back-and-forth, controlled-swerving technique that warmed and softened their rubber.

"Close up for green!" said a woman's voice in Trace's helmet radio receiver. At her command, the parade of Super Stocks sucked together like magnets. Trace wedged in bumper to bumper, wheel to wheel with the Super Stocks around him. Then the cars paired off, two-wide. To keep his hands loose, Trace waggled his gloved fingers on the small hoop of the quick-lock steering wheel.

Nudge and tap—bump and rock—the Super Stocks pushed one another like train cars rounding a tight curve.

"Lookin' good for green," the woman's voice said.

At the sudden roar of the front cars, Trace slammed the hammer down and powered up into the explosion of dust. The biggest part of any race was getting through the first turn after the green flag; he dove in hard, and pitched his Super Stock to the left—

"Whoa!" Trace yelled, and yanked the steering wheel of his car lot beater to the right. He was way over the centerline—and headed to the ditch. This was two-lane blacktop, Highway 61 north; the only left turn was into some farmer's field.

He shook his head to clear it, rolled down the window, and spit out a stale piece of gum. He let his head hang out, gulped in mouthfuls of chilly April air, then leaned back inside and took a long slug of cola.

When he focused down the highway again, Trace's own face got larger and larger in the windshield: it was not a hallucination but a Blu energy drink billboard. Trace, ten feet tall, leaned against his blue Super Stock. BLU BY YOU. FEEL YOUR POWER! the big letters read.

The billboards were all over the Midwest. He mostly had gotten past the weirdness of seeing himself on signs, but sometimes—like tonight—he got caught off guard. The whole story looped through his head: driving the snot out of his Street Stock one night at Headwaters Speedway; catching the eye of the special guest driver, Cal Hopkins; winning the Super Stock tryout; signing with Team Blu for a fully sponsored ride. Sometimes, like now, it felt too good to be true—which was the exact moment when red and blue lights lit up beneath the billboard.

"Damn!" He braked, but too late. The strobes of a cop's light bar flared across the empty highway as the cruiser pulled out behind Trace—who slowed, signaled his car onto the shoulder, then skidded to a stop.

The cop car was local, which was probably better than being stopped by a state highway patrol officer. Trace rolled down his window, then kept his hands on the steering wheel.

"License and registration?" a woman's voice asked. Her shoulder patch read DEPUTY SHERIFF.

"Sure," Trace said. "Just bought this car off a lot in Indiana. I don't have the title yet, but the papers are in the backseat."

She shone her flashlight beam into his face, then to the backseat. "Okay," she said. "Reach back and get them for me."

Trace moved deliberately as he retrieved the papers. Same with his wallet and driver's license.

She focused her light first on the purchase agreement, which seemed to pass inspection, then on his license. "Trace Bonham," she said.

"That's me." He looked fully at her, trying not to squint or scowl into her light.

"So where you going in such a hurry, Trace?"

"Just trying to get home."

"Where's home?" She looked again at his license.

Trace told her his home address—his dad's farm, in north-central Minnesota. She nodded, then glanced over the car again. "Would you mind stepping out and popping the trunk?"

"No problem."

The officer stood back as Trace got out and opened the trunk. She came alongside and skittered her beam in all corners. Except for the skinny spare tire, the trunk was empty.

"Thanks," she said. She held up his license and peered over it at his face, tilting her head left, then right, as if to see him from different angles.

"Everything okay?" Trace asked.

"Yes. Except for your speed, of course," she answered.

Trace kept silent.

She squinted at him. "I feel like I've seen you before," she said.

"That's me on the billboard back there." He gave her his winner's circle smile.

The deputy didn't blink or turn. "Say again?"

Trace repeated himself and kept smiling; this time she turned to look. Then she glanced back at him. "Stick by your car," she said. "I'm going to run your license."

He leaned against his car and waited while she sat in her squad car and looked at her computer. The night air was heavy with a chilly dampness; he shivered in his T-shirt. Inside her squad car, the deputy held a cell phone to her face as she talked. After a couple of minutes the officer came back. "You *are* the guy on the billboard back there."

"That's me," Trace repeated, mustering another winning smile.

"I called my dispatcher. Your name popped up with Team Blu racing," she said. "No wonder your face seemed familiar. I spend a lot of time parked beneath that billboard."

As Trace tried to think of something clever to say, she moved her flashlight beam up and down him. "So, are you a model or something?"

"Nope. I'm a race-car driver."

"Really?"

"Really."

"Well, considering your speed, that makes sense," she replied.

"Sorry," Trace said. "As I said, I'm just going home."

"What's the rush?"

Trace paused.

"Be honest," the deputy said. "I can be a sucker for a really good reason, but I've also got great radar for liars."

"Tomorrow night is my senior prom," Trace said. "I'm trying to make it back for prom."

"Your prom," she repeated, and narrowed her eyes. She looked again at his license.

"That's right. I drive for Team Blu, and I've been on the road, doing exhibition races—Texas, Kansas, Arkansas, last night in Bloomington, Indiana—all over," Trace explained.

"Whoa there," the patrolwoman said. "How is it you're in high school but on the road all the time, racing?"

"I do my classes online," Trace said. "It's the only way I could race full-time and still graduate."

"Okay," the officer said. "Go on."

"There's this girl back home—I need to see her," Trace continued. "Find out where we stand." Trace heard himself blurt the last part; he was way short on sleep.

"A girl. Well, Mr. Bonham, why didn't you say so?" the officer said. She handed him his license. There was a faint smile around her eyes.

Trace blinked. "I can go?"

"Just two more things. My dispatcher, Mary Jo, is a real stock car racing nut. She's not going to believe me—that you're really the billboard guy. Do you mind?" she asked. The deputy produced a silvery, pocket-size camera.

"No problem," Trace said. He leaned close to the officer, who stretched out her arm, turned her wrist—and with her thumb fired off a flash photo.

"Thanks," she said, slipping the camera back into a breast pocket. Then she pulled out her booklet and began to write.

"I'm getting a ticket?" Trace exclaimed.

"You may be on billboards, but you can't drive seventy-five in a sixty—not on my highway, okay?"

"Okay," Trace said flatly.

"I am reducing it to seventy in a sixty," she said, "but it still goes into the big computer in the sky. If you get caught speeding again this trip, the next cop is going to be very unhappy."

"Got it," Trace said. He glanced at his watch.

"Another thing: you look way better on your billboard than you do right now. I suggest you stop and take a nap—or get some coffee—or both," she said as she finished scribbling on her pad. "There's an all-night truck stop, the Highway 61, about five miles ahead."

"I'll look for it," Trace muttered.

"I might even call up there and make sure you stopped," she said, tearing off the warning ticket—*zzrrppp!*—and handing it to Trace.

"Don't worry, I'll stop."

"And one last thing," she said.

"I thought we were done," Trace said.

"Good luck with that girl when you get home."

Trace made sure to signal as he pulled back onto the highway. In his rearview mirror, the officer made a U-turn and headed back to her billboard. His billboard. Whatever. As soon as the deputy was out sight, Trace pinned the gas pedal to the carpet.

At the Highway 61 Gas-n-Go, he filled up with gas, then parked his car. Inside the restaurant, a long counter with red stools was empty. A couple of booths were occupied by late-night losers, some gothy-looking teenagers in one, and a burned-out, long-haired guy nursing a cup of coffee in another. He had used about a dozen creamers; the torn-open white plastic containers were arranged in a star shape.

Trace took a counter stool. He set his cell phone within reach.

"Hey, sailor," the waitress said as she came his way. She had pale blond hair pulled back, and a blouse with food spots on the front. "Coffee?"

"No thanks."

She handed him a menu. She was thirty-something, tired around the eyes, but had been pretty once, probably in high school. As Trace scanned the smudged list, looking for the least greasy choice, his cell phone buzzed and started to table-walk. He turned it over, checked the incoming number, then let it lie. Soon the waitress returned.

"Three eggs over hard, extra toast," he said.

She turned away and shouted to the cook.

Eating on the road was mainly a process of choosing foods that could not be totally screwed up, such as eggs and toast. Beyond those, everything was fair game for bad cooks. Racetrack food was worse than truck-stop fare; right now he missed his little refrigerator in the cabin of the Freightliner hauler—that and his comfy single bed. He let out a long breath as exhaustion hit him. He had a strong desire to lean over the counter and put down his head, but then he'd look like the rest of the late-night losers.

He went to the bathroom, took off his cap, and splashed water on his face. For a moment he didn't recognize himself in the mirror: tired brown eyes, heavy beard shadow that felt like sandpaper, cap hair that stuck out every which way. He slicked back his brown curls, which he had let grow longer lately. He wasn't superstitious, but he had won three features in the last five shows. Why change anything?

Back in the restaurant, he sat down just as the waitress brought his plate.

"Your phone was ringing," she said.

"It's always ringing," he said. He checked the number, then slipped the phone into his shirt pocket. As he bent down to eat—some protein would wake him up—the waitress remained in front of him.

"My deputy friend, Sally, tells me you were speeding tonight."

He looked up at her over a forkful of eggs. "She said she might call up here. I thought she was kidding."

"She's not a kidder," said the waitress, who was missing a tooth, upper left. "And she don't cut people much slack."

"That's for sure," Trace mumbled through a mouthful of food.

"Maybe she thought you were lucky enough already," the waitress said. She bent over and put her elbows on the counter and her face in her hands and watched him eat.

Trace took another forkful of eggs.

"You're only eighteen and you drive a race car and you're on billboards," she continued. "What's that like?"

Trace shrugged slightly. "Different," he said. He swallowed, then reached for his toast.

"Different how?"

He glanced around the diner. With any luck, some more customers would come in and the nosy waitress would leave him alone. "I'm on the road most of the time. Haven't been home for months," Trace said. "I get to eat at truck stops like this one."

"But you wouldn't trade it for anything," she said.

"That's right," Trace said.

"A lot of local dirt track drivers come in here," she said, straightening up, and wiping briefly at the counter. "They're all broke, and they all got some excuse why they didn't win their last race, but they all still believe they're gonna make it to the big time," she said. "Get a NASCAR ride and be on television."

"What's wrong with thinking that?" Trace asked.

"Nothing," the waitress said with a shrug. "Except that they put every dime into their race car, which means the family is living in some dump of a trailer—freezing in the winter, burning up in the summer—and the wife is working a second crap job and wants a divorce, and their kids are never going to college, all because their old man is chasing a dream that's never ever gonna come true." By the time she finished, her mouth was tight and hard.

Trace glanced at her wedding ring finger, which was bare.

"But hey," she said, turning away, "maybe it will be different for you."

2

He finally stopped for a nap at a Casey's Quick Stop in Soldiers Grove, Wisconsin. After a short hour slumped in the driver's seat, he got back on Highway 61 and headed north in the early morning blackness. Watchful for cops, he eased through the little towns of Viroqua, Westby, and Sparta. His route would take him north to Eau Claire, and a brief pit stop to see his mother, Sharon Bonham.

He slid open his phone and brought up MOM. She was an early bird, but it was still only 4:30 a.m. He tossed the phone onto the empty rider's seat, and kept driving. He didn't want to frighten her, but he also didn't want to surprise her by showing up at her door unannounced.

In another hour the darkness faded to predawn blue,

and in Brackett, a tiny town only twenty minutes from Eau Claire, he opened his phone and pressed her number. The phone rang and rang.

"Trace!" his mother answered. Her voice was half asleep but fearful. "Are you all right?"

"Sorry," Trace said. "I'm fine. Just wanted to let you know that I'll be stopping in Eau Claire to see you."

"Where . . . when . . . where are you?"

"Just south of town. About twenty minutes out."

"So you're stopping in Eau Claire. Just you? Your team? What's going on?" she asked. She was waking up fast.

"Just me," Trace said. "It's complicated. We raced in Bloomington, Indiana, last night, and I'm taking a little break. I'll see you soon, okay?"

"Uh, okay, sure, honey."

His mother's town house was in the central part of Eau Claire, not far from the Chippewa River. She and Trace's dad were officially divorced now, though there was some settlement thing going on that Trace stayed out of.

He parked street-side, checked his face and hair in the mirror, rubbed a finger across his front teeth to clean them, then headed toward her front door. He rang the bell; the door swung open quickly.

"Trace, honey!" his mother said. She was in her bathrobe, and she pulled him forward into a hug.

"Sorry about the time," Trace said.

"No problem. I usually get up early—as you know."

Trace could only smile.

"Are you here racing? Nearby? Are you— Tell me what's up!" his mom said.

"I'm actually taking a couple of days off," Trace explained as he came into the small living room. He flopped down on her couch—the brown leather one, from home, his all-time favorite napping couch. "I'm headed home for prom."

Her mother blinked. "Prom?"

"Yes."

"When is prom?"

Trace glanced at his watch. "Tonight."

"Tonight?" His mother seemed befuddled.

Except for the couch, her living room contained not one thing from home. With its little gas fireplace, it felt like the lobby of chain motel.

"You never mentioned that you were going to prom," she said as she turned away to make coffee.

"I just decided. Yesterday," Trace answered.

"Do . . . you have a date?"

"Nope." Trace leaned back, kicked off his shoes, and put his feet up.

His mother blinked. "Does anyone know you're coming? Like Melody or—"

"Nope. She has a date—at least that's what I hear."

"With whom?" his mother asked.

"Patrick Fletcher."

"Patrick Fletcher? He's the guy you let drive your race car at the end of last summer."

"That's right."

"Well, he's moved right in, hasn't he?" his mother said in a teasing voice.

"No kidding," Trace muttered.

Then his mother pursed her lips in one of those are-you-sure-you-want-to-do-this looks. "So you're just going to show up?" she said. "Crash your senior prom?"

"Hey, I'm not crashing it. I'm a senior there, too," Trace said.

"Even if you're taking all your classes through MOHS?" his mother asked. That was Midwest Online High School, an arrangement made for Trace by the corporate side of Team Blu.

"That's the deal," Trace said. At least he thought it was. No reason to go down that road right now. In her fluffy robe his mother appeared to have gained a couple of pounds, which for her was a good thing; even her face was fuller, but that was probably because her hair was cut shorter, and lightened, too.

"How did you find out that Melody has a date?" his mother asked. She clearly wasn't ready to let go of the prom thing.

"I still have a few friends from home," Trace said.

"Like?"

Trace shrugged. "Amber Jenkins."

"That red-haired girl driver?"

"Yes. She told Sara Bishop, and Sara told me," he said.

"Who's Sara Bishop?"

"She lives in Fargo and drives her dad's Super Stock," Trace said. "I've seen her a few times on the road, different speedways. She and Amber stay in touch. Race girls—it's a long story."

"Sounds a little like a soap opera," his mother said with an amused glance.

Trace stared at his mother. "You look good, Mom," he said, in part to change the subject, but also because it was true. He wanted to say, "You seem happy."

"Well, prom plans aside, your racing life seems to be going well," his mother said. The coffeepot gurgled as it finished.

"All exhibition races so far," Trace said. "They give us a chance to test and tune our cars. The points season starts Sunday night in South Dakota."

"That means you'll be closer to home this summer, yes?" She poured herself a cup.

Trace nodded. "Mainly tracks in the upper Midwest. Wisconsin, South Dakota, North Dakota, Minnesota, Montana, Wyoming. That's the WISSOTA sanctioning area."

"And Iowa? That's a big race state."

"Iowa is under IMCA. Different sanctioning organization, different rules."

"I've never understood that stuff," his mother said.

"It's fairly simple," he said. "Different car classes and different rules for different areas of the country. Super Stocks at WISSOTA tracks are tube-frame cars built just for racing. In Kansas and Texas and most Southern states, Super Stocks are full-bodied, factory-built cars once driven on the street."

She nodded. "Tell me about your crew. The team."

"Our engine builder, Smoky, is a genius and then some," Trace said.

"What do you mean?" his mother asked. Like mothers can, she had picked up something in his voice.

"I mean, all drivers should have such good motors," Trace said—and left it at that.

"But it takes some driving skill, too, yes?"

Trace couldn't help but smile a little. "I guess," he said.

She sat down facing him. "I have to tell you that I still feel kind of dumb," she said.

"About what?" Trace asked.

"The whole racing scene. It's a guy thing that I should have taken more seriously. It might have helped—with me and your father, I mean . . ." Her voice trailed off.

Trace couldn't think of anything good to say.

"So, better late than never, I've started to watch the Speed Channel," she said.

"No way!" Trace exclaimed.

"I like the Barrett-Jackson classic car auctions," she continued. "I have a blast trying to guess the final price of a car. Who knew that the cars from back in the day would be worth so much? The other night this '68 Dodge Charger went for over two hundred thousand dollars."

"Mom—you're turning into a motor head."

"Should have done it earlier," she said. "If I had been

on the ball, I'd have been advising my clients to buy 1960s muscle cars rather than stocks and bonds."

"For sure," Trace said.

"I also like those shows where they build a motorcycle that's one of a kind," she continued, "or else take a perfectly good car and totally customize it. But then they do that annoying father-son argument thing—nobody's getting along and the stress level is rising as the deadline approaches, and—"

"Can I have some coffee?" Trace interrupted.

She paused. "Sure! I'm sorry. You hardly ever drink coffee—I should have asked."

Trace was silent.

"And the father-son thing—I wasn't implying anything about you and your dad. I think the two of you have done all right, actually." She brought his coffee.

"Sort of," Trace said.

She patted his arm. "Better than that. Are you in regular touch with him?"

"Sort of," Trace said.

"Like, how often? About what?"

"I text him results after every race. He texts back."

"That's it?"

"Pretty much," Trace said.

Trace's mother swallowed. She stood up to wipe the counter; she always had liked clean, bare counters with no crumbs. "Does he know you're coming home?" she asked with her back to Trace.

"No."

She straightened and turned. "Are you planning on telling him?"

"Yeah. I'll call him when I get closer."

"That would be good," his mother said. For a moment she dropped her chin and let out a breath.

"What?" Trace asked.

"You want to know the main reason I watch car shows?"

Trace waited.

"They keep me close to you and your dad," she answered.

Trace went over and hugged his mother. She let him hold her for a long moment. Then she said, "I have to meet this computer tech guy at work, and you need to get on the road."

"I could use a shower," Trace said.

"I was hoping you'd say that," she said, pushing him toward the guest bath.

"Okay, I'm going!" Trace said in a little kid's voice—which brought a laugh from his mom.

After a long, hot shower, Trace came back to the kitchen. His mother was dressed for work and waiting. "School!" she said. "You have to tell me about your online classes."

Trace shrugged and sipped his coffee. "It's going all right."

"Just 'all right'?"

"I've got this teacher I've never met who e-mails me all the time. If I miss a deadline, she calls me."

"That's a good thing," Trace's mom said.

"I guess," Trace said.

His mother was silent a moment. "I think sometimes of all the things you're missing. I mean, from regular high school."

"Like sitting in a classroom bored out of my skull?" Trace replied.

"I'm sure online classes are right for some kids—" his mother began.

"For me it's the only way," Trace said, cutting her off. "I can go to school and I can race—it's all good."

"What about next year, though?" she said. "What about college?"

He shrugged. "I can do college classes online, too—or go to a real college later. Right now I need to focus on racing."

His mother paused. "When I advise my clients about money, I always recommend a diversified portfolio, not keeping all your eggs in—"

"I know what *diversified* means," Trace said sharply. "I'm not stupid."

His mother was silent a moment—as if she was counting to ten. "No, you're not stupid. All I meant, Trace, is that you seem to be putting racing ahead of your education."

"You sound just like my online school counselor."

"I like her more and more," Trace's mom said.

"Right now, racing is my education," Trace continued. "It's gonna be my career. I can go to college anytime."

His mother fell silent. "We need to have a family talk

about this—but not now," she said, glancing at her watch. "Back to prom: do you have a tux?"

"I've got a black sport coat at home. I think it still fits."

"Wear a white shirt with it," his mother said as she gathered up her purse and briefcase. "And a nice bright tie. And shave, all right?" She hurried over to give Trace a last hug. "I really have to go. Just pull the door shut when you leave. Make sure it's locked."

"Got it." He wanted to say more—that he was happy she was happy—but he didn't get it done. She was already in motion, walking quickly, carrying her slim briefcase as she headed out. After her garage door growled up and then down, Trace returned to the quiet living room. An empty house, a familiar couch—there was time for a quick nap. Just a short snooze, a half hour max. He stretched out, pulled a knitted woolen blanket over himself, and turned his face into the brown leather. It smelled faintly of home, wherever that was these days . . .

"You got enough top end?" Smoky asked in his froggy voice. Trace had gotten used to the croaky sound, but never fully to Smoky's shiny pink, earless head and his stub nose. A stock car crash and a fire had left Smoky short on head accessories. His fingers, too, were twisted and pink.

"Never enough top end," Trace called from the cockpit of the blue Super Stock.

He had won his heat at Creek County Speedway, in Sapulpa, Oklahoma. Trace's answer brought a hoarse laugh from Smoky, a guy who never asked a question unless he knew the answer. Trace had so much top-end power that he could pull any car on the track; it was as if the local Super Stocks all had one dead cylinder.

"You make it any easier for the kid, he'll forget how to drive," Harlan said to Smoky. Harlan was a burly, pony-tailed, Lynyrd Skynyrd–loving good ol' boy from Tennessee.

"We wouldn't want that!" Jimmy Joe hooted from underneath the Team Blu Super Stock. Only his jeans and scuffed cowboy boots were visible. From inside the Super Stock's cockpit, that was Trace's usual view: Jimmy's boots, Harlan's butt crack, and Smoky's dark ear hole cocked toward the engine, his pink claw fingers on the throttle linkage.

"Pump it again," Jimmy called to Trace.

Trace pressed the brake pedal. "Still soft," he called.

"Good drivers don't need brakes," Harlan said. "They race with the throttle."

"Pump it slow," Jimmy called to Trace.

Trace pressed down the pedal. The open brake line let loose a juicy fart: *pbbpbpbpbpppp!*

"That warn't me!" Jimmy called.

"Don't come out from underneath there if it was," Harlan said.

The vinegary-sweet smell of brake fluid wafted into

the cockpit, and Jimmy's wrench clinked as he rapidly tightened the bleeder nut.

Soon Trace headed out for the twenty-lap feature, which had yellow-flag restart after yellow-flag restart. Each time, the cheerful woman's voice in his helmet receiver sent Trace to the rear. She was up in the announcer's booth, the lead lap counter and position spotter (every speedway had one), who kept one eye on the cars and the other eye on her computer screen. But he didn't get angry—which clearly meant that he was dreaming all this—and it didn't matter, because after each restart he came flying back from the rear of the pack, picking off cars one by one, finding a sticky line high or low—either way—to win the feature by half a lap ahead.

At the scales, a local driver waited for him, and shook a fistful of cartoon-size green bills at Trace: engine protest. This meant a formal, by-the-rules challenge for Team Blu to prove that it was not cheating. But that didn't bother Trace, either, because nobody ever found anything out of spec with Smoky's engines. He motored off to the tech shed for the teardown. There, the chief pit steward motioned for Trace to get out of his Super Stock and lie down on the battered table. He obeyed—he had nothing to hide—and the tech guys, holding silvery wrenches and micrometers, gathered around him like a surgical team. They began removing his right arm . . .

———

"Aargh!" Trace called out. He sat up sharply and shook his right arm. It had fallen asleep, and hung on him like a dead branch. He shook it hard—it began to tingle—as he blinked away the racing dream. He was still at his mother's place in Eau Claire, but the light had brightened in the windows. He rubbed his eyes and glanced at his watch.

"Damn!" It was almost noon. He had slept more than four hours. That couldn't be right; he blinked to focus his eyes, found his phone, and slid it open. It confirmed his wristwatch reading: 11:55 a.m.

He swore again, threw off the blanket, and stood up, doing some math on the fly. He was still six hours from home. In the best case, he would arrive with prom ready to get under way.

3

Sixty miles north of Minneapolis, the shimmy in his right front tire grew from teeth-chattering to car-shuddering. In the center console, Trace's can of cola slowly came to a boil—brown foam oozed onto the seat and floor. He drove slower and slower.

Finally, he wheeled into a gas mart parking lot, then got out and popped open the trunk. The skinny donut of the spare tire was hard to the touch—fully inflated. So far so good. He lifted out the tire and then unfolded the flimsy jack and extendable cranking rod. Before jacking the out-of-balance front tire fully off the asphalt, he fit the tire iron onto the first nut; loosening lug nuts required some back friction on the tire. However, the first nut didn't loosen. As he leaned into it, the whole car torqued backward—and threatened to tip off the undersize jack. Trace positioned the tire iron horizontally, then stood up and pressed down onto it with his shoe. Nothing. He put both feet on the skinny iron rod—balancing himself against the hood—then bounced. The car rocked, but the nut remained frozen. He swore for real this time.

"It's a conspiracy," a woman's gruff voice said.

Sweating, Trace glanced up.

"Car companies and tow truck drivers—they're in cahoots," she said. Paused beside her pickup was a middle-aged woman in a faded brown Carhartt jacket and black stocking cap pulled low. She was holding a gallon of milk. "They tighten those nuts down with an air wrench. That way you have to call a tow truck."

"No kidding." Trace breathed deep. Her face was weathered—had seen a lot of sun and wind. She was clearly an outdoorsy type. Trace tried again, bouncing atop the tire iron.

"I hate to say it, but you're either going to strip the stud or break an ankle. Then you're for sure not going to get that tire changed."

Trace stepped down. He pursed his lips. Just what he needed, a peanut gallery.

"I think I've got some WD-40 in my toolbox," the woman said, opening her end gate. "There might even be a torch in there—if there's any gas left in it."

"That would help," Trace said. He wiped sweat from his face.

The woman secured her milk, then climbed into the

junk-filled rear of her truck, an older Ford F-150. She rummaged around in the diamond-tread toolbox, then turned and tossed a blue spray can with a red top to Trace. Digging deeper, she came up with a small propane torch.

"Great," Trace said as he sprayed the four frozen nuts, then let the fluid penetrate. The woman climbed down, produced a cigarette lighter, and with a *pop!* lit the torch.

"I'll do it," she said, motioning for Trace to step aside.

"Okay." He wiped away the excess penetrating oil, and moved back.

She knelt by the wheel. "A lot of young people nowadays ain't good with cars," she said, squinting as she moved the shivering yellow point of the flame from one nut to the next. "Not their fault," she added. "It's the auto industry and the politicians. They're in bed together, too. They try any way they can to cut people off from understanding their own cars—and being able to fix them."

"Maybe so," Trace murmured. He checked his watch. This pit stop was getting way too long.

"They've got us by the throat with most every car built since about 1996," she said, working her flame back and forth. "A 'check engine' idiot light shows up on your dashboard, and you got to go back to the dealer. They plug your car into their computer, and half the time there's nothing really wrong. It's something like 'Check the check engine light,' but they still charge you seventy-five bucks."

"Let me try those nuts now," Trace said. He didn't have time for this.

She moved aside. Trace fit the wrench to the first nut, which loosened like a spoon twisting in warm butter.

"You can buy those handheld computer code readers," she said. "But the dealers don't want to share their codes. They won't tell you what the numbers mean."

Trace quickly spun off the last nut, jacked the car higher, and swapped tires. On the skinny spare, he tightened the nuts snugly in a crisscross pattern. Then, after lowering the car, he wrenched them tighter.

"Somebody taught you how to do that right, at least," she observed.

"Thanks," Trace said, though she didn't pick up on his sarcasm.

"Anyway," she said, and spit to the side, "what this country needs is a true people's car. Like the Volkswagen Beetle. That was the whole idea—a car that anyone could drive and anyone could fix. In German, *Volkswagen* means 'the people's car'—did you know that?"

"No, I didn't," Trace said, in his car by now. He fired the engine.

"It was one of Hitler's ideas," the woman said. "Not many people know that, either."

"Gotta go," Trace said, yanking the shifter into gear. He accelerated away. The world was full of crazy people, but at least this one had tools.

The wheel shimmy was gone, and Trace concentrated on making up time. North of Little Falls, he ducked off Highway 10, the main route northwest, and took Highway

64 up through the woods. It was a narrow, two-lane black-top with pines close up on both sides. There was less chance of highway patrols here, but more chance— Which is exactly when a whitetail buck bounded up from the ditch. Head up, horns erect, it raced across on a collision course. Trace went into deer-whack mode: he lifted his hands off the wheel and closed his eyes. It was his personal—maybe crazy—solution to a deer on the highway. He would either hit the deer or not hit the deer, but at least he wouldn't swerve to avoid it, go off the road, and end up as a mangled tin-can sandwich in the trees.

When he opened his eyes, the highway was empty ahead. The white flag of the deer flashed once in the side mirror, and then was gone into the gray pines. He let out a breath and put the pedal to the floor; a near-miss usually meant at least a few miles of deer-free driving.

The sun was fully down by the time he drew near Headwaters, population 9,274. As always, the parking lot of the smoky old Eagles Club south of town was full of cars and trucks. An auto consignment lot across the street had doubled in size since he'd been home. It now had a section that included snowmobiles, ATVs, and fishing boats—even a couple of tractors. Which reminded him: he had forgotten to call his father, but later on that. Right now he pulled his Team Blu cap low over his forehead, slouched down in his beater, and headed west to the high school.

The parking lot was jammed. The cars and pickups

were shinier than usual; everybody on a date had detailed their ride. He spotted two familiar vehicles right away: Beau Kim's dropped black Honda Civic and Amber Jenkins's dusty Chevy pickup. He did not see Mel's white Toyota. Then again, why would it be here if she had a date?

He parked his car at the far end and headed to the main entrance. In the foyer was a table of PTA adults.

"Excuse me!" one of the women said quickly. She was one of those supertidy mom types, the kind who totally overparent their kids.

"Yeah?" Trace said. He had tried to slide by, as if he hadn't noticed the table full of sign-in sheets and plastic wristbands.

"This event is for high school students only," the woman said. She sat up straight in her chair, her eyes wide and unblinking. Pager in hand, she was in full stranger-danger mode.

"I am a high school student," Trace muttered.

"At this high school?" the woman asked. The other chaperones stared at him.

"Sort of."

"Do you have your ID?"

Trace fished through his wallet and found his old school ID. In the photo he was clean-shaven and had short hair.

"Trace Bonham?" she asked. At his name there was a murmur from the table.

"Yes. That's me."

The woman stared at his ID, then at Trace. "Would you mind taking off your cap?" she asked.

"Yes, I would mind," Trace said.

"Trace!" said a man's high-pitched voice from behind. It was Mr. Jorgenson, Trace's ninth-grade history teacher.

"Mr. Jorgenson. Hey."

They shook hands, after which Trace grabbed back his school ID.

"What a surprise! I'd heard that you left us for good," Mr. Jorgenson said as they moved past the table toward the gym.

"Nope, just back for a visit," Trace replied.

At that moment, Mr. Jorgenson's pager chirped— clearly he, too, was on security detail. "Gotta run," he said, and turned back to the foyer. Trace was left alone to walk down the wide hallway toward the music and colored lights.

He took a breath, then stepped into the doorway. The basketball gym had been transformed into a giant cruise ship. The back wall was papered and painted to look like a wide blue ocean. The prom theme, in giant letters, was "Sail Away!" Little sandy islands and palm trees receded into the distance. At the base of the fake horizon was the ship's railing made of pipe, where kids leaned and sipped "drinks"—probably pink lemonade. In the foreground was a ballroom and casino with adults dressed up as blackjack dealers, all the better to spy on the kids. Above the dancing and gambling throngs, the long arms of the retractable basketball hoops were ringed with black construction paper in order to resemble big smokestacks. Actual puffs of "smoke" came from the pipes.

"Oh my God! Trace? Trace Bonham?"

He turned.

A short, round-faced girl, probably in ninth or tenth grade, and dressed as a cocktail waitress, paused beside him. She carried a tray of pink-colored drinks.

"Yeah?"

She squealed, and the tray of drinks tilted—Trace grabbed the front edge to steady it. Faces turned briefly toward the doorway, but the deejay's sound track covered her breathless voice.

"I can't believe it. I heard you're going to be on TV? Or in a movie? With your race car!"

"No," Trace said. "I just drive the car."

"I love those billboards with you leaning on your car," she said in a rapid-fire gush. "Some of my friends have them as wallpaper on their computers, and nobody famous has ever come from this school!" She began to hop up and down, her drinks slopping over onto the tray.

"Be cool!" Trace said, trying to keep his voice down.

"Could I have your autograph?"

"No, not now," Trace said.

"Please?" Her chirpy voice lifted toward a shriek.

"Okay, okay!" Trace said. He had a pen, and looked around for something to write on. She set her tray on the floor and leaned in close.

"Here—on my arm," she said, holding out the inside of her forearm.

"This is a ballpoint pen. It might hurt," Trace said.

"Like I care?" the girl said with a giggle.

Trying not to pierce her skin and tattoo her with ink, Trace signed his name. As he moved the pen, he said, "Do you know Melody Walters?"

"Who doesn't?" she said.

"Is she here?" Trace asked as he finished.

The girl, beginning to bounce again, pointed to a cluster of tuxedoed boys and formally dressed girls crowded around a blackjack table. Tudy and Leonard, both looking sharp, were the center of attention; Leonard, in an all-black tux, was shaking dice, ready to throw. He looked very lucky tonight.

Then Trace squinted beyond them, and saw her—white strapless dress, blond hair up in elaborate swirls. In her heels Mel was over six feet tall.

"Thanks," Trace murmured. When he turned back, the girl was rapidly thumbing her cell phone—which meant he had to move fast. He took off his cap, sucked in a deep breath, and stepped onto the gangplank made of two-by-fours.

He headed straight to Mel's group. Patrick Fletcher stood beside Mel. His right hand rested on the small of her back, but she was turned away from him as she laughed and talked to a group of girls also in gowns and with high hair. Mel held a large corsage of pink flowers.

The other girls saw Trace before Melody did; one by one their mouths froze around their last words spoken. They began to poke one another with their elbows. Suddenly Mel's laughing voice was the only one in the group. She turned to look over her bare, tanned shoulder.

"Hi," Trace said.

Mel's eyes went from smiling to stunned.

Patrick turned, too. His eyes widened, and his hand dropped from Mel's lower back. She wore eye shadow and pink lipstick, and her upswept hair had fine flecks of glitter, some of which had fallen into the delicate white ridges along her collarbone, and farther down, onto the soft swell of her very white cleavage. Her face turned pale—as if all the blood had suddenly been sucked from her cheeks.

"Trace!" she whispered.

"Hey, everybody," he said, and flashed a smile.

"Whoa! It's Trace!" Patrick said, rocking back as if hit by an invisible shock wave. He pretended to collapse into the arms of another guy—which brought a giggle from the girls. All except Mel. Her gaze stayed locked on Trace.

"Why are you— What are you trying to do?" she finally said, her voice shaky.

"I didn't want to miss my prom," Trace said, glancing around. "Last-minute decision. Left Team Blu, bought a used car, and drove home."

"Left Team Blu for good?" Patrick asked. He seemed taller, bigger, than last summer, and he finally had some blond chin whiskers of his own.

"Are you kidding?" Trace said, purposefully not looking at him. "This is only a visit."

"Well, lucky us," Mel said.

There was dead air. Patrick took the lead. "Come on, guys, let's pick it up here. Trace the famous race-car driver is back!" There was an edge of sarcasm in his voice.

The whiteness of Mel's face turned slowly into blotches of color on her neck.

"How could you do this?" she asked Trace.

"Do what?" Trace asked. The girls around Melody had pulled in tighter—like bodyguards—and glared at Trace.

"You truly don't get it, do you?" Mel said, her voice recovering its strength, and color rising up into her cheeks.

"Get what?" Trace asked.

Mel walked away, still clutching her flowers. The cluster of girls swirled protectively behind her, and escorted her through a decorated, sheeted-off area called "Sail Away Powder Room—Ladies Only."

"Well, that went fairly well," Patrick said, trying to make a joke.

"What do you know about it?" Trace growled.

"Know about what?" Patrick said.

"Her," Trace said. It was the only word left in his head at this moment.

Patrick stared. "Are you, like, stoned or something?"

Trace grabbed Patrick by the cummerbund.

"All right already!" a girl's voice called. Amber Jenkins came hustling over, unsteady in high heels; she was strapped into a pink dress with puffy shoulders, and her hair was pulled upward and frozen in place with shiny spray and glitter.

"Hey, Mr. Big," she called, and pulled Trace away from Patrick.

"Hey, 13a," Trace said, and got a big hug. Amber drove a Mod-Four at Headwaters Speedway, but tonight she was in full girl mode: she smelled good, plus had some serious cleavage going. Tugging her front up, she balanced herself on her high heels. "Aren't you supposed to be in Iowa tonight? That Super Stock invitational thing?"

"Yeah." Trace looked around for Patrick, who was angrily straightening his cummerbund.

"We keep track of you, you know," Amber said, holding on to Trace's arm. "Sara Bishop sent me your racing schedule." A couple of other girls nearby ditched their dates in order to join Trace and Amber; quickly Trace became the center of a growing circle.

Beau Kim shouldered his way through the ring of kids. "Don't tell me, dude—you lost your ride!"

"No way," Trace said. Kim, another Mod-Four racer at the local speedway, was with a cute younger girl Trace didn't know.

"He came back to check up on Mel," Amber said, trying for a joke.

"Just call me the Placeholder," Patrick muttered.

Trace ignored him. "Actually, I didn't want to miss seeing all of you in your monkey suits."

"Says the monkey!" Beau shot back. There was good-natured jeering at Trace's street clothes.

"What, can't afford a tuxedo?" someone asked.

"You look like you just came from the pits," Amber said, rubbing at something on the side of his face.

"Uh, Trace? Could I get your autograph?" Beau Kim's date asked. Her voice fell dead center into a moment of silence between songs. She held out the prom-night program.

"His autograph?" Beau said to her.

"Yes, why not?" the girl said. She looked at Beau.

Among the circle of kids, it was like someone had hit a giant Pause button.

"What is wrong with you?" Beau asked his date.

The girl snatched back her hand as if she had been stung.

"Wait—it's okay. No problem," Trace said.

Beau's date set her chin defiantly as Trace took the program and pen from her. "See?" she said to Beau.

"Will you sign my program, too?" asked another girl—and then another. Quickly a cluster of giggling girls formed around Trace, which was the moment when Melody and her attendants returned. Mel, still clutching her corsage, looked like she had finally found the right words for Trace—until she saw him signing autographs.

"Great!" she said. "Just freaking great!" She wound up like a baseball pitcher and threw the corsage at Trace. The fastball of pink carnations was high and outside. It hit another girl's tall, lacquered swirls of hair—and tipped the big pile sideways. The girl shrieked as the collapsing hair fell over onto her right ear; she whirled around, swearing, as she looked for whoever had ruined her hair.

"Plus I hate these shoes!" Mel shouted. She took off her high heels and pitched them high and far, for maximum distance. First one and then the other crashed into the papered horizon of blue-green waves. Big sheets tore and peeled, falling of their own weight, revealing the concrete-block gym wall behind.

Things went downhill quickly after that. Adults homed in, corralled Mel, and hustled her in one direction; other parents broke up the group around Trace, escorting him out into the hallway. Behind, on the sinking cruise ship, the music played louder and faster—something to dance to.

"This one is gone. He won't be coming back tonight," one of the adult blackjack dealers announced to the table of foyer guards.

"I knew he was trouble!" the tidy woman at the table said. She narrowed her eyes at Trace.

Beau, now dateless, said, "We came to steal your daughters, and we'll stop at nothing!" He leaned in to make a face at the woman.

"All right, that's it!" said a couple of dad types working security. Within seconds, Beau and Trace were pushed out the door—ejected into the cool spring night—and the door slammed shut behind them.

Trace and Beau looked at each other.

"All in all, that went fairly well," Beau said.

"Yeah, right," Trace said. From inside the gym came the muffled disco beat, then the long, low sound of a ship's horn.

"Someone must have seen an iceberg," Beau said. "Céline Dion's gotta be next up on the sound track."

They looked around. The parking lot was quiet; there was no sign of Mel.

"Want to cruise for real?" Beau asked.

"Why not?" Trace said with a shrug.

He squeezed into Beau's tricked-out Civic, and settled back as Beau accelerated away from the parking lot. The exhaust pipe's big collector can hummed *Wha—whaa—whaaa—whaaaaaa!* as he went through the gears. The stereo woofer in the trunk thudded like thunder.

"I got a bottle in here, too," Beau shouted.

"I could use a drink," Trace shouted back.

"Not that kind of bottle," Beau said. Watching his rpm, he reached down and flipped a toggle switch—and the Civic punched forward as if it had been slammed in the rear end by a logging truck.

"Whoa!" Trace called.

"Nitrous!" Beau said. "Cold air intake, turbo, 4-2-1 header, custom can by Tenga—this baby's got it all."

"What's it do in a quarter mile?" Trace asked.

"Around fourteen seconds flat," Beau answered.

"That beats a lot of V-8s," Trace said.

"Tell me about it," Beau said. "Off the line, they hole-shoot me big-time—then think they've got it in the bag.

About the time they let off, I get all ricey on them, and shoot past them like they're standing still."

"Sweet," Trace said, "but don't get us killed, all right?" They were doing ninety.

"Good point," Beau said, and backed off. "The goal in life is not to be a cliché."

"Huh?" Trace said.

"Like stalling the car on the railroad tracks on prom night? That sort of cliché."

"Or being an Asian kid who drives a rice burner," Trace said.

Beau looked at him.

"Hey, it's true," Trace said.

"Yeah, well," Beau said, cracking a smile. He down-shifted sharply into a U-turn, and headed back toward the city limits sign.

"So what else have you got under the hood?" Trace asked.

As Beau went into four-cylinder tech talk, Trace checked his phone.

"As if she's going to call you," Beau said.

Trace looked out his side window. "I should have let her know I was coming."

"A little late now," Beau said, downshifting once more. They drove down Main Street, which was mostly empty. "I probably should head home, check in with my old man," Trace said. "It's been a while."

"Okay," Beau said. "I'm going to drive around until I

find some V-8 sucker to hustle. Lots of them in this town."

"If you see her, call me," Trace said.

Beau dropped Trace back at the school, chirping his tires as he left the parking lot. Trace listened to him go through his gears, then turned to his own car. On the way home, he called his father.

"Trace! What's up?" his dad asked.

"Nothing. Well, not nothing. I'm in town."

"Town? What town?"

"Here. Headwaters."

There was silence. "Aren't you supposed to be in Oskaloosa tonight?"

"Yeah, well, it's a long story."

"Holy moly. You didn't—"

"No, I didn't lose my ride," Trace said. "I'm just taking a night off. I came back for prom."

There was murmuring in the background. His father's voice came back, louder this time. "Prom? You never said anything about coming home for prom."

"Kind of a last-minute thing," Trace said.

"Ah, okay," his father said.

"Anyway, I'll be home in about ten minutes."

"Ten minutes? Ah, okay, great. See you soon, kid."

Kid. His father never called him "kid." What was up with that?

"Okay," Trace said. He shut his phone, shrugged, and headed northwest out of Headwaters and into farm country.

The Bonham farmstead had a wide yard, fronted on

the west side by shiny grain bins, then the long machine shed on the south. Trace's house, a modern rambler, was tucked behind a windbreak on the north.

Parked by the house was a Corvette, a nothing model, early 1980s, with a door dent. His father hadn't said anything about a 'Vette.

Trace parked and went inside. He did not bother to knock, but actually thought about it—which was a little strange. It still was his home.

"Trace!" his father called. He came across the room in jeans and T-shirt, barefooted, and gave Trace a hug. He smelled like a woman—perfume of some kind. Women and booze.

"Well, hi again, Trace," came a woman's voice. It was Linda, his dad's girlfriend. She was wearing one of Trace's shirts—a white one—and not much else that Trace could see. Her hair was wet.

"For God's sake, put some clothes on," Don Bonham said as Trace pulled away.

"I have clothes on." Linda giggled. "I found this nice shirt."

"More clothes!" Don said. He stalked across the room, grabbed her elbow, and spun her around, then pushed her out of sight down the hallway. He turned back to Trace. "I'm really sorry."

Trace shrugged. "Hey. I guess it's Saturday night." He turned to the refrigerator, which had a half loaf of bread, lots of beer, some pickles, and a big block of stinky cheese.

"Hungry?" his father asked quickly.

"Not really," Trace said.

"That cheese is not for everyone, but it'll grow on you," he said.

"Looks like it's already growing," Trace said.

"Have a beer, then," his dad said. "Unless you're going out again."

Trace paused. From the rear of house, probably his parents' bedroom, Linda was singing.

"We're kind of partying," his dad said. "I wish I had known . . ."

"Yeah, I meant to call," Trace said. "I didn't know you had a roommate."

"Linda doesn't live here," his dad said sharply.

"She seems pretty well at home," Trace shot back.

"Hey, I need a life, too," his father said. "Your mother and I—"

"I gotta go check on some things," Trace said. "I'll be back later."

"Wait, don't go!" his father replied, reaching out, but staggering.

Trace brushed off his father's hand. "Don't!" he said—his voice loud and sharp, just like his dad's. Within a minute, he was speeding down the driveway.

4

Trace headed back toward town. He wanted to stay off the main drag—if Beau saw him, he would think Trace had ditched him—and there was no future in going back to the high school. He made a pass down Main Street, looking for Mel's car. As if she'd be cruising tonight. With nowhere to go, his steering wheel turned him east, toward Headwaters Speedway. He knew this short drive by heart, and it felt strange heading that way without his old Street Stock swaying on a trailer behind.

The speedway was dark except for pale moonlight, which created shadows on the huge humps of dirt, and on heavy dirt-moving equipment—scrapers, bulldozers, and graders. As track manager for her dad, Johnny Walters,

Mel had been talking about upgrading the track for two years—her goal was to bring back sprint cars, the kind her father used to drive—but Trace and most other drivers never thought it would actually happen.

The speedway gate was open; he drove inside. Quietly closing his car door, he walked across the torn-up parking lot to the old wooden arches, and then into the grandstand. Inside, there was just enough moonlight to see the track—which was clearly wider now, and its corners taller. He stepped onto the dirt. Reaching down, he gathered up a clump and sniffed it: earthy, soft clay that squeezed into a ball. No more sand. No more stones working up through the gravel to break a steering rack or ring a driver's bell when they spun up and whacked him in the helmet visor. Car counts had been falling every year at Headwaters because of the increasingly rough track. He pitched the clay ball toward the new, high-banked turn 1.

Which was when he heard something.

He looked around.

There was only silence.

He listened longer. A small, swallowed sound came from up in the grandstand, near the announcer's booth. For a moment he thought it was a night bird—an owl of some kind—but then he realized it was a hiccup. Someone trying not to hiccup.

"Hello?" he called into the shadows. He headed up the worn wooden steps toward the announcer's booth. Mel was sitting there in the dark.

"What are you doing here—" she said, finishing with a hiccup.

"I'm not sure," Trace said.

She was silent. He could see the white side of her face and her silvery ponytail and lots of white papers on the desk. It looked like she had been working, and then turned out the lights when she heard a car. Her prom dress was gone, and she was back in normal speedway clothes—jeans, sweatshirt, and racing cap. On the road, whenever he thought of her—which was every day—she looked exactly like this.

"Well, I can tell you one thing for sure: you made a complete ass of yourself at prom," Mel said.

Trace was silent. "It was really stupid—I mean, not letting you know I was coming."

"The whole prom thing was stupid. I will never put on high heels for a boy again in my life," she said.

There was a long silence. A really long silence. "I know how to get rid of hiccups," Trace ventured.

"Like what—scare me? Well, you don't—*hiccup!*—scare me, sorry."

"No, not that. You have to get the air out of your stomach. It's sort of like that Heimlich thing, but slower."

"What, are you—*hiccup!*—a doctor now, too?"

"Just trying to help," Trace said.

Her chair scraped, and she came to the doorway of the shack. "All right. I'll try almost anything."

"Stand up and face the track," Trace said. He stood

behind her and looped his arms around her belly. She smelled like peaches and hair spray and summer.

"Now what?" she asked.

"Now I'm going to slowly squeeze upward on your belly while you bend forward."

She actually followed his instructions—and burped. She straightened up and broke away from his arms. "That's it?"

"We'll see, won't we?" Trace said.

Mel sat down on the bleachers and stared off at the track. They were quiet for a long time, which was a good sign. No more hiccups.

"You looked so different," she began.

"Different? Like how?"

"Older. Like a man. When you showed up at prom, I didn't recognize you. That's what upset me."

"Hey, I'm the same guy," he said.

"No you're not," she answered. "I know about race-car drivers."

She meant race-car drivers and girls—fence bunnies (as Harlan called them).

"I don't do that," Trace said. He should have said, *I try not to do that.* But that part didn't come out. He turned away, as if to survey the speedway. "The track is going to be great."

"Yes, it is," Mel said, coming over to stand close beside him. She looped her arm through his.

"It's going to be a whole different speedway!" Trace said.

"You thought I couldn't make it happen?" she teased.

"No. Not that," he said. "It's just a way bigger deal than I imagined."

"Like me," she said.

"Yes, like you." He turned back to her; she pulled him down beside her on the wooden bleachers.

"This whole grandstand is going to be demolished," she said, touching the worn wood. "New aluminum bleachers with seat backs. New concession area. New johns."

"Sounds great," Trace said.

"Let's hope so. This whole thing has to work, or the bank and some investors aren't going to be happy with me," Mel said, looking across at the construction equipment.

"It's gonna make it," Trace said quickly. "Drivers are going to love the new track, and it starts with that. Once you have the drivers—once the car count is up—the fans will follow." There was excitement in his voice.

Mel was silent. Then she said, in a softer voice, "I was surprised that you came here to the track tonight."

"Yeah, well, my options were kind of limited," he replied.

She stared at him.

"I went home, but my dad has a girlfriend. They were pretty drunk."

"Oh dear," Mel said.

Trace shrugged. "Adults. What can you do?" he said flatly. He leaned back on the bleachers and looked up at the moon. So did Mel. The moon had a large bite out of its right side.

"There's a word for that," Mel said.

"For what?"

"For which way the moon is scooped out, but I can't think of it right now."

"Don't ask me," Trace said. Their elbows touched as they leaned back farther.

"Remember last summer when you took me to the gravel pit to see the meteor shower?" she asked.

Trace nodded.

"I really screwed that up," Mel said.

"No you didn't."

"Don't lie. I did. And you know what?"

"What?"

"When I got home, I stayed up late, and you were right—the Perseid meteors started shooting across the sky one after the next. They were unbelievable."

"I stayed up, too," Trace said, turning to her. "I saw them."

"We just didn't wait long enough," she said.

Suddenly they were kissing—hard, hungry, bruising kisses. They made out like crazy, until the bony edges of the wooden bleachers dug into their backs.

"Wait," Mel said, breaking away. "Come." She led him inside the announcer's booth, where it was much darker, and they fell into an old easy chair—a recliner—that smelled like cigarettes. There they went by feel. All-over feel, their hands everywhere at once, until they were breathing hard. Mel suddenly pushed him away. "Don't move," she said.

He obeyed.

She stood up. There was soft rustling, then the brief tearing sound of a zipper, then more rustling. As his eyes adjusted, moonlight slowly pooled in two perfectly round planets, swimming toward him, growing more distinct—or else he was jetting toward them at warp speed through the blackness. The quick glint of Mel's teeth—she was smiling—flashed like a shooting star, and he reached for her. Her skin was fragrant, and shiny, as if the moonlight was inside her. With her help he peeled off his shirt—but a minute later Mel sucked in a breath and stiffened in his arms.

"What?" he whispered.

"I . . . can't," she breathed.

"Why not?" he groaned.

"This would be my first time."

"Yeah?" he said too quickly. "I mean, are you scared?"

"No. I've always had this dream—about me and you—that our first time would be someplace really nice."

"Like?" he said, trying to buy time, holding her close, continuing to stroke her long, smooth bare back.

"Like, in a hotel, with a big feather bed. And candles. And a Jacuzzi. And chocolates and champagne."

"That's really girly," he said.

She giggled, and kissed his ear. "A smoky old announcer's shack and a wrecked-up chair—that wasn't in my fantasy."

"It works for me," he said—pretending to be joking.

"I want to," she said quickly, "but not here. Not tonight. We need to plan ahead."

"Tomorrow night?" Trace said.

"No, dummy." She laughed. "Plan ahead ahead. Like meet someplace out of town. Spend the whole weekend together."

"The whole weekend?" Trace said.

"Why? Does that scare you?"

"No. It's just that I race most weekends," he replied. It was a stupid comment; he felt their big moment slipping away.

She was silent. "This summer, then," she said. "We need to wait until this summer. We'll both be done with school then, and things will feel totally different—and I'll be totally ready."

"This summer?" Trace began. Mainly he was thinking about punching himself in the face for being so dumb.

"Think you can wait that long?" she asked softly, blowing warm air into his other ear.

Trace swallowed. "No problem."

She giggled.

After they put themselves back together, they headed to Perkins. It was three a.m. by then, and the place had only a few kids in prom clothes; most were at all-night, lock-in-type parties. Trace and Mel ordered major breakfasts—omelets and pancakes.

"You two sure are hungry," the waitress remarked.

"No kidding," Trace said, which brought a smile from Mel.

Then, as they ate and hung out, they talked. Mel told him about the racetrack, about school, and about Patrick.

"We're just friends," she said.

"Maybe in your mind," Trace mumbled.

Color came back into Mel's cheeks. "So why didn't you ask me to prom?" she said. "You came back. You could have planned ahead just a little bit, and not turned the whole thing into a soap opera."

Trace looked down. "I wish I could do it over."

"Anyway," Mel said, "let's talk about you."

"What about me?" Trace replied.

"What it's like with your crew? Racing. Being on the road all the time."

Trace glanced down briefly, then told her the main parts about being on the road: Harlan, the crew chief and full-time huckster for Team Blu; Jimmy, the Xbox king and Super Stock setup guy; Smoky, the team motor man. He didn't tell her about Sara Bishop, whom he talked to a lot—mostly about racing. Or April, the college girl from North Dakota, whom he had met at a speedway concession stand.

"Have you had any more engine protests?" Mel asked; the first one had been at Headwaters last summer.

"Yes," Trace said.

"And?"

He shrugged. "We always pass inspection."

She cocked her head. "You don't seem all that happy."

"I miss working on my own engine. I like to know exactly what's in there."

"You're a pro driver now," Mel said. "You can't do everything."

"I suppose you're right," Trace said without enthusiasm.

"Do you see much of that creepy Laura from corporate headquarters?"

"She's not that creepy," Trace replied quickly.

"Yes she is. I don't trust her."

Trace laughed—then saw that he shouldn't have. "Don't worry. She's way too old for me."

"I would certainly hope so," Mel said. "And what else aren't you telling me?" she teased.

"That's pretty much it. Racing, then hanging out in my little cabin, thinking about you."

"Yeah, right."

Trace was silent.

"Sorry," Mel said. She leaned against him. "I believe you."

"Let's talk about this summer instead," he said.

Mel blushed slightly.

"When does summer officially begin?" Trace asked, stroking the backs of her hands with his thumbs.

"According to the calendar? Or according to me?" she said.

"According to you," Trace said.

She pulled her hands away. "The Fourth of July," she said, color coming into her cheeks. "That always feels like summer to me."

"I'll bring some fireworks," Trace said. "I can get real ones down in South Dakota."

"I don't think we'll need any fireworks," she said.

They hung out at Perkins until dawn, and then left in separate cars. Mel went home. Trace headed to South Dakota to catch up with Team Blu.

5

Trace arrived at the Dakota State Fair Speedway in Huron, South Dakota, not long after the pit gates opened. Heats started in two hours. He parked across the pit fence from the Team Blu hauler, staggered out of his car, and hurried to the gate. His pit pass was waiting.

Inside the pits he walked past a lineup of race-car trailers and haulers, their stock cars unloaded and pointed toward pit row. Team Blu's Freightliner hauler was buttoned up, the Super Stock out of sight. Smoky's mini–motor home, an older Gulf Stream camper with a Ford nose, sat alongside the hauler; its roof bristled with antennae, including a small satellite dish. Smoky always parked so he could watch the track from his side window. Harlan lounged in his lawn chair beside the tall blue Freightliner like a security guard for a Southern rock band.

"My, my, my—look what the cat drug in," Harlan said. He wore his usual Team Blu T-shirt with the sleeves cut off to accommodate his beefy arms, along with sunglasses and a red do-rag. He was having a cigarette. At the sound of voices, the trailer's side service door opened a crack; Smoky, like a Team Blu trailer troll, peered out, with Jimmy Joe's narrow face popping up briefly over his shoulder.

"Don't ask," Trace said to his crew.

"You're lucky we didn't change the lock on your cabin," Harlan said.

"Sorry," Trace mumbled. That was all he could think to say, or explain. His butt was dragging, big-time.

"But hey, I've been there," Harlan said with his Tennessee drawl. "I once drove straight through from Tennessee to California to see a girl—and she was married."

"How'd that turn out?" Trace said.

"Don't ask," Harlan said.

A raspy laugh came from Smoky.

Jimmy Joe stepped outside, wiping his hands on a clean grease rag. "Yep, we've all been there," he said cheerfully to Trace.

"Who's this 'we'?" Harlan asked. "I've never seen you drive any farther for a girl than the nearest high school parking lot."

"He picks them up in Wal-Mart," Smoky said, hacking at his own joke.

"Anyway," Harlan said to Trace, "Laura from headquarters is pissed that you missed that promo thing at Oskaloosa."

"Pissed pissed?"

"I think so," Harlan said. "She's sending Tasha down here to talk to you."

"No big deal. I'll work it out with them," Trace said.

"Maybe I should work it out with them," Jimmy Joe said, checking his fingernails on one hand and then the other.

Harlan spit. "Those girls are so far out of your league you couldn't get a date with either one of them if you had a NASCAR ride."

"Speaking of rides, what are you gonna do with that car you bought in Indiana?" Jimmy asked.

Trace shrugged. "I hadn't thought about it."

"I'll take care of it," Jimmy said.

Trace tossed him the keys. Jimmy Joe was Trace's half friend, half assistant. He was in his early twenties, slender but wiry, with sandy hair cut in a semi-mullet. He bunked in Smoky's motor home, while Harlan took the Freightliner sleeper cab.

Harlan squinted at Trace's dusty car lot special. "How long you did you drive on that skinny spare?"

"Since Minnesota," Trace said.

"What did I tell you, Pops?" Jimmy said. "Trace is one lucky guy."

"But lucky in love? That's the question," Harlan said, and drew on his cigarette. There were guffaws from the crew.

Trace was already inside his cabin, peeling off his stinky clothes on his way to the shower.

"One hour in the sack, max," Harlan added, his voice muffled by the wall. "You can sleep when you're old."

Trace awoke a minute later (it felt like) to thudding on his cabin door.

"Visitor," Harlan called.

Trace groggily checked his watch, then staggered out of bed. He had slept for less than an hour. He pulled on jeans and a T-shirt, then opened his door.

"Ouch!" Tasha said. She was Laura's assistant from the Minneapolis office, a cool, twenty-something woman originally from Chicago who shifted his gears every time he saw her. She looked him up and down.

"He's all yours," Harlan remarked to Tasha, and headed down the short stairs.

Trace tried to slick back his hair. He and Tasha had a brief hug, but it was not the full-body kind she usually gave him.

"What's up?" Trace asked.

"What's up? You blew off that exhibition race and promo shoot in Iowa, so I had to drive down here and chew your butt out. That's what's up." Tasha was always fairly direct about things.

"Had to go home, sorry," he said.

"The one thing that Laura hates—and me, too—is when people don't keep to the schedule. It's sort of a thing all the way up the chain at Karchers and Ladwin Agribusiness—the name you see, of course, on your paychecks."

"Sorry," Trace said.

"Sorry doesn't cut it," she said. "About eighty percent of life is showing up."

He and Tasha usually had a good vibe between them, but not today; she was all business.

"It won't happen again," Trace mumbled.

"It had better not. Anyway, how was prom?" Tasha asked, her voice softening just a bit.

"A disaster," Trace said.

"They usually are. And Mel?"

"She's great."

"Worth the trip?" Her voice was teasing now.

"For sure," Trace said, blushing slightly.

"Boys," Tasha said, and clucked her tongue. "Can't shoot 'em, can't live without 'em. Anyway, I'm gonna let you do your race thing, but we still need to talk later. A little matter of Sheila from MOHS."

"Damn," Trace said, and turned down the corners of his mouth.

"Exactly," Tasha said, her voice serious again. "But nothing we can't handle—if you get your act together."

"Time to saddle up, kid," Harlan called from below in the trailer. "Heats start in less than an hour."

"So later, all right?" Tasha said. "I'll catch the feature from the stands, then see you after the races."

When she was gone, Trace splashed cold water on his face, then pulled on his racing suit and headed downstairs. At floor level in the long hauler, Smoky was leaning over a carburetor on the stainless-steel bench. He wore a surgical-type headlamp with a light and a magnifier lens. In his bent, stiff fingers was a voltmeter or something similar; it had red and black probe wires.

"Whatcha doing?" Trace asked.

Smoky jerked the carb behind him, out of sight. "I'm doin' what I'm doin'," he croaked. He turned to Trace and kept his hands behind his back.

"Just asking," Trace said.

"You drive, I take care of the car, remember?" Smoky asked.

"Sure," Trace said with a shrug. "I just drive." He passed by Smoky and out into the warm spring air.

"It's a long third-mile track," Harlan explained as they walked toward the entrance. "Not all that high-banked, so Jimmy's got your front suspension pretty tight, and quite a bit of toe."

Trace nodded, but he was counting Super Stocks as they walked along pit row. Eighteen so far.

As Trace and Harlan moved along, the energy of a speedway gearing up for racing began to pulse inside him. The exhibition season was over. Tonight the summer points chase started for real, and the pits were a carnival of activity. Brightly lettered fluorescent graphics and decals made the cars look fast even standing still. On his knees beside a battered Modified, a pit man flapped a floor jack handle like a one-winged bird trying to fly. A dust-bunny teenager bounced a freshly mounted tire— *poom-poom-poom*—toward a waiting hub. At the rear of a black Super Stock, a scruffy guy poured blue-tinted fuel into the red hummingbird nose of a deep-throated funnel. The sweet scent of 110-octane racing fuel hung in the air. Farther down the line came the sharper, nose-biting odor of methanol exhaust. It mingled with the burnt smell of smoking black rubber worms that fell from the tire-siping irons, and the odor of the concession shack's deep-fat fryer, which was clearly in need of an oil change. Air tools chattered, tire irons clanged, generators hummed, grinders rasped as crew members roughed up new tires for better bite. Country music twanged from one race-car trailer; heavy metal pounded from the next. The big-cat snarl of a Chevy engine came again and again as a motor man blipped his throttle linkage, and announcements— broken up by all the other noise—crackled intermittently over the pit loudspeaker.

"Indiana was red clay, South Dakota is black dirt—but not heavy gumbo," Harlan said. They were on the track now, and Trace kicked at the clumpy soil. The big sheeps-foot roller, pulled by a tractor, had left its uniform pattern of pockmarks—which would be pressed full soon enough by the pounding of race-car tires.

"Jimmy's got a new siping pattern he thinks is right for

your rear tires. If you don't like the bite, let me know," Harlan said.

"He's usually right when it comes to rubber," Trace said.

"I hate to agree," Harlan said, and spit; he was proud of Jimmy in a gruff kind of way.

Trace looked around. Other than their dirt, speedways were pretty much the same: grandstand, infield, pit area either in the infield or to the side, and concessions. Dakota State Fair Speedway had a cluster of grain elevators just across the railroad tracks, and open fields behind. As they turned back toward pit row, Trace and Harlan paused to let a race rig rumble past. A shiny Ford pickup pulled an open trailer with an orange Super Stock swaying on top. The decals were local ones from Norfolk, Nebraska.

Trace looked twice at the kid riding shotgun in the truck. A small dude with a buzz cut and brown eyes, but the cauliflowered ears and slightly bent nose of a wrestler. It was Jason Nelson, a high school driver who had run strong in the Team Blu tryouts. He signaled to his father, who braked their truck and trailer.

"Howdy," Jason called to Trace. He had a weirdly deep voice.

Trace lifted his chin.

"How's it been going with Team Blu?" Jason asked.

"Good," Trace said. "Lots of travel. All exhibition races so far."

"But points tonight," Jason said.

"That's right," Trace said.

"How's the track look?" Jason asked.

"Fast," Harlan said.

Jason grinned. "Just the way ah like it."

"Me, too," Trace threw back.

"Gotta go," Jason's dad said gruffly. "We're running late today." He let his eyes travel over the Team Blu hauler.

"See you out there," Jason said to Trace, and the Nelson rig rumbled forward.

"That kid's a driver?" Harlan asked.

"And then some," Trace said. "He's fast."

"He looks like he's in fifth grade," Harlan said.

The evening's Dakota State Fair Speedway Invitational lineup included five classes: Limited Street Stock, Street Stock, Midwest Modifieds, Modifieds, and Super Stocks. The more expensive Late Models were on their own circuit, and had less flexibility to attend special race nights like this one.

"Super Stocks run last," Harlan said, reading Trace's mind.

"Which means a dry, slick surface," Jimmy added, "but I'll have you set up for it."

"They don't pay you enough, Jimmy," Trace said.

"Hear that, Pops?" Jimmy crowed.

"Yeah, yeah," Harlan answered. "Who's the one who drew a number 95 for Team Blu?"

Jimmy instantly looked hurt. "Trace wasn't here yet, so you told me to do the draw."

"Should have had Smoky pick for us," Harlan said.

Smoky was a gambler who loved to stop at every casino they saw.

"Well, Trace has got his work cut out for him," Harlan said. "We start in the fourth row, outside, third heat."

"Dead last, in other words," Trace said.

"Yep," Harlan said.

"Hey—no problem," Trace said. He walked alone over to the pit bleachers to watch the Street Stock classes. The beat-up, full-bodied old Monte Carlos rocked and rolled around the track, their slush-bucket suspensions tilting the battered bodies through the turns, their motors straining to pull them down the straightaway. Last year that had been him—no sponsor, a flatbed trailer, a run-what-you-brung racer. Standing beside the fence were the pit crews, the fathers, and a couple of motor head mothers; they cheered, pumped their fists for their cars, their drivers, their kids. They slapped one another on the back, laughed, swore, bummed cigarettes, paced. Grassroots racers. That part of racing would never change.

Another thing that never changed for Trace was his prerace nerves. On race day he was always hungry because he couldn't eat until after the races. Driving a stock car was no different from being a basketball player, a football player, or any kind of athlete. The closer it came to race time, the more the butterflies came alive inside his stom-

ach and fluttered their tickly little wings. He headed back
to his crew.

Jimmy came across the pits pushing a hand truck that
carried a white, square-sided fuel jug; blue racing gas
sloshed inside. Most race teams bought their fuel on-site
from a centrally located parts depot—which also carried
tires, tubes, fuel filters, and air filters, as well as basic suspension parts that racers tended to break, such as shocks,
front and rear springs, and tie-rods. Smoky waited in the
small doorway of his trailer. Jimmy hoisted up the fuel jug;
Smoky lifted it inside, then closed the door.

"We should carry our own drum of fuel," Jimmy said,
wiping sweat from his forehead. "Wouldn't have to buy it
and lug it around."

"It's dangerous to have a barrel of gas in the hauler,"
Harlan said. "Let's say we're at a red light and some crazy
ass in a Kenworth is asleep at the wheel. He rear-ends us,
we go up like a bomb. Trace's cabin would be ground zero."

"Great," Trace said.

"Plus if you carry your own fuel, the other drivers
think you're cheating," Harlan said.

"Hey, we got ourselves a bang-up driver—we don't
need to cheat," Jimmy said cheerfully.

Harlan was silent. From behind the closed door of the
hauler, where Smoky worked, came the faint clinks and
thuds of tools.

Trace glanced at his watch. "Are we going to see the car
pretty soon?" he asked. All the other race cars sat beside
or behind their haulers, poised to go.

"When Smoky's ready," Harlan said.

That was not for another half hour, when the Midwest Mods—the class just before Super Stocks—were already under way. Smoky finally appeared in the little doorway and signaled to Jimmy Joe, who hustled inside and powered open the tall rear door of the stacker trailer. Then, with a handheld controller, he winched the lower Team Blu Super Stock backward down its ramp and into daylight. The car was immaculate, as always—the prettiest Super Stock in the pits. Having a second car on the stacker rack above was the ultimate luxury for any dirttrack racer: if Trace wrecked one night, they were ready to go the next night with the second car. They could not, of course, switch cars between a heat and a feature—a standard rule in racing.

Trace slid into the narrow cockpit feetfirst—right foot, then left—and got settled. Harlan handed Trace his helmet and gloves, then went to work cinching Trace's six-way seat-belt harness, neck brace, and sternum protector. The aim was to be one with the full-containment racing seat. Driving a stock car was not for people who were claustrophobic.

"I need to breathe," Trace muttered as Harlan tugged the shoulder belts still tighter.

"You can breathe after the race," Harlan said.

Once his gloves and helmet were on and secure, Trace gave a thumbs-up sign to his crew. "Fire in the hole," he called. He flipped the toggle On switch, then touched the rubber starter button.

RRRRRuupppp! The big Chevy engine coughed and caught—then settled into a rumble. As Smoky leaned over the long front nose, Trace blipped the throttle a couple of times. Smoky listened, then nodded and pointed toward the track as if to show Trace where to go; it was an odd little ritual, but it was theirs. Every team had them.

Trace's heat included Jason Nelson in the second row outside. Glints of orange, like late sunlight through leaves, were all Trace could see of Nelson in the pack. As the drivers scrubbed their tires in a rumbling, weaving parade, Trace breathed deeply in order to stay loose.

"One lap to green," a woman's twangy voice said through his helmet receiver. Trace rocked his steering wheel to make sure the quick release was secure, then fell into line down low. A silvery local Super Stock, No. 69— the racing world's least original race-car number—tucked in alongside him. Trace ignored him, and made a point of keeping his nose tight against the car ahead; he was loaded, locked, and ready to pull the trigger.

At the green flag roar, he let No. 69 surge forward, then cranked across his rear bumper to the outside. He took a high line through turn 1, but held back when No. 69 swung his butt sideways, taking up two lanes. Trace had been there before; drivers liked to tap the front corner of a trailing car just enough to make it squirrelly—or send it bassackwards off the track. The resulting yellow flag was usually ruled the fault of the car that spun out. Any driver who caused two yellows was done for the night, so there was no reason to take a chance on receiving the first yellow.

After a couple of laps, traffic spread out, and Trace went hotfoot. He pulled No. 69 and another car on the high side, and, in the eight-car heat, dove into fifth place—close enough to see Jason Nelson, who was now leading the pack.

Heat races were only ten laps (sometimes less), and Trace worked hard to get into third place by the time the white flag waved. He had a shot at second place, but didn't want to risk a wreck or a spinout; the goal, always, was to get to the feature race with the car in one piece, so he streamed under the checkered flag comfortably in third place.

After crossing the scales, he rumbled up beside Jason Nelson, who had stopped his No. 77x for a checkered flag photo. Trace braked, nodded his way, and Jason pointed back; it was a courtesy moment among racers. Then Trace spun his tires and headed to the pits—where Harlan beckoned him toward the trailer's rear ramps.

Tracc killed the engine. Even before Trace got out, Jimmy had hooked up the cable and was ready to winch the car inside.

"What?" Trace said.

"Smoky wants to check over the engine."

"Runs fine!" Trace said, loosening his neck collar.

"Smoky didn't like something," Harlan said.

Trace shrugged and climbed out. He was only the driver.

Harlan and Jimmy had a few questions about how the car handled, after which Trace walked over to the small pit concessions to get a bottle of water. He was standing in line when Jason Nelson walked up to him. Nelson was munching on a nacho platter swimming in bright orange cheese.

"I expected to see you on my ass there at the end," he said.

"No rush," Trace said. "It's a long season."

"Most teams run out of money before the season's over," Nelson said, "but I guess that won't happen to you."

In the feature, Trace and Jason Nelson lined up bumper to bumper, with Jason behind. Both were well back in the twenty-two-car feature. Some lineups put faster cars farther back to make them work their way up through the pack. This prevented a follow-the-leader type of race—a single line of cars chasing one another's tails—which was boring for everybody, especially the fans.

Jason Nelson clearly didn't plan to be stuck behind Trace for long. On the slow lap before green, he wedged his nose underneath Trace's bumper and kept it there like a tow truck trying to push-start a car. Trace swore, and rode his brakes. His rear end lifted partway, and his back tires lost bite.

"No. 77x—back it off!" said the woman's voice.

Trace's rear end settled groundward, but it was hard bumpety-bump until green.

At thunder-up, Nelson quickly swung around Trace on the high side. Orange tin lurched tight alongside and stayed there—until the corner. The track was always shorter on the inside line, and Trace pulled most of a car's length in front of Nelson. Down the straightaway it was the same story: Nelson came alongside but couldn't make the pass, then lost ground in the corner. Each lap, the blue and orange Super Stocks powered down the straights as if welded side to side. This kept up for three laps, with Trace pushing Nelson slightly higher each time.

On lap 4, Trace came up too fast on a white Super Stock, and made a split-second decision to go high—and pinch Nelson onto the marbles. Nelson knew enough to stay off the drier, pebbly rim of the track; he braked and knifed low, sliding by the white car on the inside. Then he squeezed the white car's line—forcing him upward, toward Trace. Trace thought he was safely past the guy, but the white car's nose clipped Trace's rear quarter panel. Tin crunched—and knocked Trace loose. He cranked the wheel wildly right, then left to avoid spinning out, and by the time he found his line again, Nelson was out of sight ahead. Trace had fallen back several places and now ran in the last third of the pack. By the time he picked off some cars to reach the middle of the pack, it was already lap 10—which was when his engine came alive.

Trace felt it. It was nothing obvious, like Beau Kim's nitrous bottle kicking in, but more like what a near-miss crash did to the heart rate. His tach reading jumped 300 rpm; on the floor he suddenly had another half inch of pedal. Something had let loose—probably one or more piston rings—and when this happened, the pistons ran freer in their cylinders: it was the surge just before the engine blew. Trace glanced behind, expecting a cloud of blue smoke—oil blowback—but there was only dust and stock cars. His instinct was to back off and save what was left of the motor, but that was last year talking. This year a fresh motor was ready to go in the Blu trailer. He kept the hammer down.

The Super Stock engine found its sweet spot, and Trace pushed it to the limit. He took a high line for a couple of laps, pulling cars like they had fallen out of gear, then played down low, looking for daylight toward the front of the pack. Nelson's orange tail, bright as a monkey's butt bouncing through the jungle, came up quickly. He was running third.

A spinout somewhere behind brought out the yellow flag, which positioned Trace on Nelson's back bumper for the restart. Rather than play bumper cars, Trace gave Nelson a half-car length of breathing room.

"Try me," Trace said inside his helmet.

Nelson fell for it: on the restart green, he faked an engine lag—a moment's hesitation—that was really a tap on his brakes. Since there were no brake lights on race cars, who was to know? It was an old trick: sucker the driver behind into a rear-ender, and in the process make him slice a front tire or break a tie-rod. A yellow flag usually resulted. As in real-world driving, the race car that rear-ended another was at fault—and got sent to the back or, worse, into the pits.

But Trace was waiting for it. He swung low at the same moment that Nelson braked—and came past him on the inside as if pitched forward from a giant slingshot.

"Sucker!" Trace shouted as he broke through the dust into first place—where no one came close to him for the final five laps.

After the race, Trace crossed the scales and then proceeded to the victory circle. Only the photographer waited. None of the other cars paused to salute him. Trace emerged backward through his window and pumped an arm to the stands. There was scattered clapping from this South Dakota crowd—Tasha cheered loudly—but also scattered boos and jeers from the cowboy hats.

"Cheater!" someone called. It was picked up by several other voices in the stands. "Cheater! Cheater!"

The photographer, a fat guy with thick glasses and a pale face, handed Trace the checkered flag and knelt down for the photo. "Folks here don't like you much," he said from behind the camera.

Trace fixed a smile on his face. "No big deal," he said, not breaking expression.

After the photo, Trace headed to the tech lane, where he pulled in behind the other four top-finishing Super Stocks, which were going through inspections one by one. His engine was hot, and Jimmy waited with a fire extinguisher full of water. Trace kept the rpm up while Jimmy sprayed the radiator. Thin jets from the silvery can—their squirt gun—hissed into clouds of steam; slowly the temperature-gauge needle drifted down out of the red. "We're good!" Trace called, and Jimmy stepped back from the hot fog, his face speckled with watery mud.

The other cars were finished with brief inspections. A tech guy bent down to Trace's window. "We'd like to see you in the tech shed," he said, and pointed.

Trace shrugged and drove forward, turning left into a metal-roofed garage. Bright lights came on to greet him.

"Take the lid off," the main tech said to Jimmy. Harlan, close by, was chewing a toothpick.

Jimmy quickly unpinned the hood; he and Harlan lifted it free. The tech guys gathered around. One removed the air cleaner and shined a flashlight into the throat of the carb; another guy worked the butterfly choke. The tech guys operated in silence except for the *clink*s of small wrenches. After a couple of minutes, they stepped back without comment.

"Next we'd like to look at your valves," the chief tech man said.

"You might as well relax," Harlan said to Trace. "Looks like it's going to be a while."

Jimmy was ready with a small socket and ratchet; he removed the valve covers. The tech guys bent over the exposed valve springs and rocker arms, which were shiny with warm oil. Using micrometers as well as a feeler gauge, they measured clearances. After a few minutes of this, they straightened up and stepped back, poker-faced. "Looks okay," one of them said.

"Yeah, well—I never seen a Super Stock run like that," said a voice from the side. It was Jason Nelson's father. Jason, still in his racing suit, stood beside him.

"Me neither," the chief tech guy said to Harlan. "So we're going to pump a cylinder. See what you've got."

"Have at it," Harlan said.

"Let's do number 4," the tech said to Jimmy, who bent over and spun out the spark plug of cylinder number 4. As he worked, he looked up at Trace with nervous eyes; Trace flashed him a thumbs-up. Beside Jimmy, Harlan removed two rocker arms so the valves to cylinder 4 would remain tightly closed, then loosened the ignition coil wire so that the engine would turn over but not start.

"Okay. Do your thang," Harlan said, stepping back.

A tech guy came forward with what looked like a complicated bicycle pump; it had a short nose, a screw-in nipple, and a graduated tube with a disk inside; its purpose was to measure cubic inches of air—the displacement of a cylinder. After twisting the gauge's nose into the spark-plug hole, the main tech man nodded to Trace—who touched the starter button and turned over the engine.

The guy squinted at the volume reading. "Again," he called.

Trace obeyed.

After three revolutions of the motor, the tech guy held

up a hand. "We're at 44.95," he announced. "Times eight cylinders, that makes"—there was a pause as he did the math—"359.6 cubic inches."

"There you go," Harlan said. "No way we're over 360 inches."

The tech chief leaned in to read and confirm the cylinder displacement, then turned to Harlan. "Next we're going to take a fuel sample."

Harlan's lips tightened slightly. "Like I said, have at it," he said with a shrug. He moved to the rear of the Super Stock, took off the smaller, back lid, and removed the gas cap from the fuel cell.

A tech approached with a handheld device that looked like a meter reader; it was attached to a small, silvery container the size of a coffee cup.

"Octane analyzer," Harlan said to Trace. Harlan took off his sunglasses. With pale white eye sockets and squinty eyes, he looked smaller, less certain.

The gas guy pumped fuel into his container, then set the whole device on a stainless-steel counter and punched some buttons. Several tech guys gathered around.

After a few moments, the gas man turned toward the car. "It's 109 octane," he said to the chief tech guy. "The rule is 110 or under."

"Well, hell—we paid for 110 octane from your speedway supplier," Harlan said as he put his sunglasses back on. "We should get a discount."

"Don't press your luck here," the main tech guy said evenly.

"Anything else?" Harlan asked.

The main tech guy looked at Trace and the blue Super Stock, then turned to Harlan. "Not at this time. But we still don't like the way your car ran away from everybody," he said, wiping his hands on a clean rag.

"No legal Chevy motor runs like that," Jason's father muttered.

"Money talks and bullshit walks," Harlan threw back at the older Nelson. "Next time protest our engine. We'll be happy to take your money."

"Okay—we're done here!" the chief tech said, and motioned to clear the building. "You're free to go," he said to Trace.

When Jimmy and Harlan had finished putting the top end back together, Trace fired the Super Stock motor and chirped his tires on the way out of the tech shed.

Back at the trailer, Tasha was waiting. "What was that all about?" she asked.

"What, the tech inspection?" Trace said as he pulled himself upward through the window.

"No. That stuff over in the stands."

"You mean, people not so happy that we won?" Harlan asked.

"Yes," Laura said. "The 'cheater' thing."

"Local cowboys," Harlan said with a dismissive wave. "They root for the hometown racers, and they hate it when somebody from out of town takes their money."

Trace was silent.

"Hey, kid—our first feature win of the season!" Harlan

said. He threw a beefy arm around Trace. "Did y'all see his move on the last yellow flag?"

"Yes. Pretty cool," Tasha said.

"He's the real deal," Harlan said. "There's plenty more checkered flags where that one came from."

From the hauler came the faint sound of Smoky closing his little window.

6

For their meeting, Tasha joined Trace in his cabin. She sat on the pull-out couch; Trace leaned back on his bed.

"So," Tasha began.

"I know, I know," Trace said. "I'm behind at MOHS."

"The Phantoms," Tasha said. "It's a sweet name for an online high school mascot, but from what I gather, you've been taking it literally."

"We don't have to show up," Trace replied.

"You know what I mean," Tasha said. "Your counselor tells me that you haven't been turning in your online work, you won't take her calls, you don't respond to her e-mails."

"I've been racing a lot," Trace began.

"Don't kid me," Tasha said. "At most you race three

times per week. You've got lots of off-hours while you're
traveling. What are you doing with all your time?"

Trace shrugged.

Tasha looked around his cabin. Her gaze went to his
gaming collection and his Xbox. She reached over and
picked up two empty cases. "GTA IV. Warhammer," she
said. "Great."

"Jimmy and I play some," Trace said. "He's good."

"What does that tell you?" Tasha said.

Trace shrugged again.

"He's a good gamer because he plays a lot. Because he
plays a lot is why he's a tire and setup guy," Tasha said.
" 'Proficiency at pool is a sign of a misspent youth.' "

"Pool?" Trace replied.

"It's an old saying," Tasha explained, "but nowadays it
would probably be gamers, not pool players." She tossed
the disk cases to Trace.

He caught them. "I'll get on it," he said.

"I'll get on it," Tasha said, mimicking him. "You sound
just like my younger brother, Caleb, back home. He's a big
basketball stud in high school. All he does is shoot hoops.
Doesn't leave home without a basketball—he's constantly
dribbling it between his legs or rolling it up and down his
arms and across his shoulders. He's silky smooth. Scouts
been watching him since grade school."

"He must be good," Trace said.

"Way good," Tasha said. "So good my whole family's a
nervous wreck about it. You know that movie *Hoop
Dreams*?"

"Heard of it," Trace said.

"It follows these two kids who can throw it down—I mean, they're both really good—just like Caleb. One of them sort of makes it, at least to college ball. The other kid gets injured, gets into drugs—a really sad story."

There was silence in the little cabin.

"I've been thinking that you're in that kind of movie now," Tasha said. "Except it's stock car racing, not basketball."

"You're saying I'm not going to make it?" Trace asked.

"I'm saying you gotta watch the lifestyle part," she said. "You can't just race cars, play video games, and sign girls' T-shirts."

Trace looked down.

Tasha leaned forward. "You need to be more than a one-trick pony."

"Okay, I hear you," Trace said.

"This thing we got with Team Blu is business, and business can change just like this." She snapped her fingers with a sharp *pop!*

"I'm on it—I promise," Trace said.

"Good," Tasha said, standing up. "That's what I wanted to hear. Now, enough of this—you already got a mother and I'm not her."

"That's for sure," Trace said.

Tasha paused at the door, the faintest of smiles around the corners of her lips. "I'll bet you never saw many girls like me at your school."

"None," Trace said.

"Well, honey, everything they say about older women is true," she answered. "But I'd never even consider hooking up with a guy who couldn't finish high school."

Trace fell back on his bed as her footsteps thumpety-thumped down the stairs. He let out a long breath, and lay there a couple of minutes, getting his wits. He thought about stepping into his little bathroom and bleeding his pressure valve (as Harlan called the act) but, on second thought, stood up and went to his little window. He wanted to get one last glance at Tasha, who looked great from the front or the rear.

She was still in the pit area. A Ford pickup and trailer carrying an orange Super Stock had stopped on the way out. Tasha stood with one hand on the truck's roof as she leaned in. She was talking with Jason Nelson.

7

Harlan powered the big blue hauler out of the Huron speedway as soon as the Super Stock was tied down and the trailer buttoned up. Team Blu would not race again until Saturday night in Billings, Montana, with a promo stop in Gillette, Wyoming, on the way, but Harlan liked to get gone.

They had been under way only a few minutes when there was a light tap on Trace's cabin door. He looked up with surprise. "It's open."

Jimmy poked in his head.

"Harlan take off without you?" Trace asked. Jimmy usually rode up front with his dad; there was no inner door between the hauler and the tractor's cab.

"Yeah. He hates hanging around after a race."

"No kidding," Trace said.

"Says that after you win, only bad things can happen if you stick around—but I think he was scared of the cowboys," Jimmy said with a yuk. He swayed in the doorway as the truck turned.

"Want to shoot some trolls?" Trace said, nodding toward the Xbox.

"Better not," Jimmy said. "You're supposed to be doing your homework."

"I'll get it done. Take a load off," Trace said, nodding toward the couch where Tasha had sat. "I can never do much of anything right after a race."

The Speed Channel was on, and they watched a show where drag strip fans guessed the quarter-mile pass times. Jimmy cleaned up; he was always within a couple tenths of a second. During a commercial break for new cars, Trace turned suddenly to Jimmy. "Hey—what'd you do with my car?"

"I met this girl, a single mom, at the concession shack," Jimmy said.

"And?" Trace said.

"I gave it to her."

They watched the next two cars do their burnouts— then power down the straight track. "Seriously, what did you do with the car?" Trace asked.

"I told you—I gave it to her," Jimmy said. "Handed her the keys and the paperwork. 'It's yours,' I said."

"What'd she say?"

" 'Thanks,' " Jimmy said.

"Is that all?" Trace asked.

"Well, not exactly," Jimmy said, and blushed.

Below, Harlan shifted gears.

"I figured she needed it more than us," Jimmy said.

Trace looked up, as if he could see or smell something. "We're heading south," he said. "I can feel it."

"Could be," Jimmy said.

"Aren't we going to Montana?" Trace asked.

"Yup," Jimmy said. "Pops is dropping down to I-90 and then west."

They were silent for a while. "You could spin me around blindfolded and I would always know my directions," Trace said, his eyes on the next pair of drag racers.

"That's another skill I don't have," Jimmy said.

"You got skills," Trace said.

Jimmy shrugged. When he was away from his father, he was way more serious—a different guy altogether.

"Want some food?" Trace said, gesturing to the fridge.

"No thanks. Got plenty of comp food for myself, Pops, and Smoky from the concession girl."

"I would hope so," Trace said. "What else did she give you?"

Jimmy's narrow shoulders bounced with silent laughter.

The truck's engine pulled one more time, then settled back into high gear and lower rpm, as if the highway was clear ahead.

"The car ran great tonight," Jimmy said.

"And then some," Trace said.

They were silent for a while.

"How'd you meet Smoky?" Trace asked.

"Pops knew him. He was a driver out of Corbin, Kentucky," Jimmy said. "In the sixties, before NASCAR came down on everybody with rules and template bodies, he raced with the big boys, like Jimmie Johnson—until he crashed."

"What happened?"

"He was racing asphalt, a long-distance thing at Darlington or someplace like that. One of those races where the more fuel you can carry, the better. Drivers would come up with tricks to hide extra fuel in their cars—even one gallon could make the difference between winning and losing. Some guys welded up little minitanks here and there; they say Smoky might have had race fuel inside the pipes of his roll cage. All the tubing full of fuel. He never said that, but I guess when he crashed, his car went off like a bomb."

Trace sucked in a breath.

"He was in the hospital so long, people forgot about him," Jimmy said. "People thought he was dead, which was all right with Smoky. It allowed him to disappear, until Pops ran across him working in the back room of a filling station as a mechanic. People kept talking about this guy who could fix anything—especially Chevy motors. He could make 'em sit up and bark, they said. Pops was starting to race himself then. Smoky built him a motor, and they just hit it off."

"How old is he?" Trace asked. It was good to get Jimmy talking; he knew stuff. He was way smarter than he acted.

"Sixty at least. Maybe close to seventy."

"I thought he was, like, fifty," Trace said.

"You should see pictures of Smoky before he got burned. Brown, curly hair. Big chin and nose. He could have been in the movies," Jimmy said. "He says he'll never get wrinkles because his skin's burned tight."

"Does he have family?" Trace asked.

"Nope," Jimmy said. "We're it. He's sort of like a granddaddy to me."

Trace was silent.

"He's taken a real shine to you," Jimmy said. "Says, as a driver, you remind him of himself back when he was young and bulletproof."

"Are you kidding?" Trace said, turning to Jimmy. "He won't tell me anything. Keeps all his stuff locked up. I've never been inside his trailer."

"It's pretty full in there," Jimmy said quickly. "He's got all this electronic stuff. Hardly room to turn around."

"What kind of electronic stuff?"

"Beats me," Jimmy said, his eyes flickering sideways. "I'm just the tire and setup guy."

"All those antennas and stuff. It's like he could run a radio station," Trace pressed.

Jimmy's phone beeped. He gave it a quick look. "I better go or Pops will think I'm bothering you," he said to Trace.

"You don't bother me," Trace said.

Jimmy grinned shyly. At the door he paused, then said suddenly, "You want to know something funny?"

Trace waited.

"I'm a crew guy on a race team and I don't even have a driver's license."

"You get in trouble and lose it?"

"Nope. Never got one. Never took the test."

"Why?" Trace said.

Jimmy shrugged. "I was afraid. Still am."

"Of the test, or what?"

"Sort of."

"You can read, right? I've seen you."

"Yeah. But slow. Sort of like my typing."

"At the testing place I think they have people to help you with that part," Trace said.

"It's not the reading part. I just freeze up in general. I can't do tests."

"You could pass both parts easy," Trace said. "It's not like you can't drive."

"That's what Pops tells me. I keep telling him I'm gonna do it, but then at the last minute I get the shakes and I chicken out. I'm twenty-two years old and don't have a driver's license—ain't that sad?" he said with a laugh. He turned to leave.

"What are you going to do down in the trailer?" Trace asked.

"There's always stuff to do. Clean up. Sweep. Or I'll just sit by the car," Jimmy said.

"You can stay here."

"Naw. Pops wouldn't like it."

The following two days, Trace chipped away at his MOHS assignments. They didn't take long once he set to work; it was starting that he hated.

He got permission to write a research paper on the concept of the Volkswagen. His adviser, Sheila, thought it was the "perfect" topic for Trace, being that he was a car guy—though she asked him to make it more than just research. "Make it an argument," she e-mailed.

"Huh?" Trace typed back. Team Blu was parked at a Wi-Fi rest stop near Spearfish, South Dakota.

"Not an argument argument, where people are shouting at each other, but a logical argument. As in making a case for one side or the other," she replied.

Teachers—they were never satisfied with the original idea.

"What sides do you mean?" Trace typed back.

"Make one up. Take a position for or against. For example, that 'people's car' issue that you mentioned—it's a good thing or a bad thing, depending on your personal interest."

"It's a good thing," Trace wrote.

"There you go," she replied. "And don't paste big chunks of stuff off the Internet. Do most of your research there if you have to, but the writing has to be your own. If you borrow something and use it, be sure to cite where it came from."

"Yeah, yeah," Trace muttered.

"And one more thing," she wrote. "One of your sources has to be an actual book or magazine article that you found in an actual library."

"How am I supposed to do that?" Trace typed. "I'm on the road all the time."

"Where are you now and where you headed?"

"Spearfish, SD–Billings, MT," he wrote. When she didn't reply right away, he Googled "Hitler and Volks-wagen." A ton of stuff came up instantly: the crazy Car-hartt lady had been right. Trace clicked on one article about Hitler meeting with Ferdinand Porsche in 1933 to talk about a "people's car." Porsche designed the small car, then started his own company after World War II.

Trace's e-mail icon flashed. It was his teacher, sending the addresses of the public libraries in Gillette, Buffalo, and Sheridan, Wyoming, along with Hardin and Billings, Montana.

"Here you go. Any one will do! ☺ Sheila."

"Cute," Trace muttered. "No need. Just found every-thing I need online," he typed back.

"Online research is overrated. In your citation put the name of the librarian you talked with—in person—and the phone number of the library."

"Okay!"

After Sheila went away, Trace scanned through on-line articles, looking for facts and key quotes that he could use, and trying to avoid wacko sources. One site had "proof" that Hitler was still alive and had designed the Hummer.

In the middle of this, the Freightliner rumbled alive. Trace grabbed his cell phone.

"Can we hang here another half hour or so?" he said to Harlan. "I'm doing my homework online and I need the wireless."

"How'd people do homework before the Internet?" Harlan grumbled.

That night, Team Blu stopped at the Wal-Mart parking lot in Gillette, Wyoming. As usual, Smoky tucked his little motor home tight alongside the Freightliner. They all ate together at a Denny's; as usual, Smoky wore his wrap-around sunglasses and Bardahl cap. Trace was used to the glances that waitresses and people nearby sneaked at Smoky, but when they gawked, Trace made it a point to stare back at them.

"It's all right. It don't bother me," Smoky said to Trace.

"It does me," Trace said.

Smoky's narrow, scarred mouth turned upward in a part of a smile.

After supper Harlan and Smoky headed off to a casino. Jimmy came up to the cabin and played Xbox while Trace worked on his paper.

"I wish I could type," Jimmy said after a while. "I just hunt and peck like a damn chicken."

"They've got sites online, with timers to check your speed," Trace said.

"Timers?" Jimmy looked over at Trace. "Whoa."

"You don't have to use them," Trace said. "It's not a test—they're just for practice."

Jimmy returned to giving his thumbs a serious work-out.

Trace pushed ahead on his paper, getting most of the writing done, and even a start on the bibliography page. After an hour, he powered down and grabbed an Xbox controller. They played until three a.m., when Harlan and Smoky came back laughing and bumping around and cheerful.

"Pops must have won ten bucks," Jimmy said. His phone beeped. "I gotta go," he said quickly.

The next morning Trace's cell phone rang just after ten a.m.

"Two-hour warning," Harlan said. He, too, sounded groggy. "We got our mall thing at noon. And remember— Laura wants you suited up."

"Got it," Trace mumbled. He turned over in bed.

"We don't want any more trouble from headquarters," Harlan said.

Trace closed his eyes and drifted back to sleep— waking up when the engine rumbled alive and the air brakes hissed. He took a quick shower, pounded a small carton of orange juice, then got dressed. It felt weird putting on his racing suit when there was no race. Embarrassing, actually. Like the suit was not a suit, but a costume, and he was an actor.

Trace grabbed his cell phone. "What?"

"Whooo-ee! Look at this," Harlan said as he braked the big rig.

Trace stepped to his porthole window and peered out. A mall was a mall, and a parking lot a parking lot—but in the center of this one were blue flag banners stretching in a giant half circle, with a Team Blu billboard erected as a backdrop. A bright blue refrigerated truck, medium-size, sat waiting.

"I guess we're in the right spot," Trace said.

"Show-and-tell time," Harlan said. He eased the Freightliner into the lot and slowly up to the billboard and the Blu beverage truck.

Trace headed down into the trailer, where Jimmy was unhooking the Super Stock's tie-downs. When the car was cable-ready, Jimmy opened the service door. There was a sudden commotion outside—girls' giggling voices—and Jimmy jumped back into the trailer and slammed the narrow door behind him. "There are people out there!"

"Yes," Trace said. "This is a mall."

"No, I mean, girls."

"Girls are good."

Jimmy's phone beeped. "Okay, okay!" he said, no doubt to Harlan. Jimmy took a breath, and headed back outside.

A minute later there was rattling at the rear of the

hauler. The electric motor hummed, and the tall door, like the ramp of a castle lowering, let a flood of sunlight into the trailer. Trace shielded his eyes. As his vision focused, faces came into view—a couple dozen young girls, middle-schoolers, began to shriek.

"Trace! Trace!" they called.

"Hey," Trace said.

"Over here," Harlan called to Trace.

There was a table set up next to a kids' swimming pool (blue of course) filled with ice and Blu energy drinks. Trace headed down the ramp, and the giggling girls crowded around.

"Here you go! Free stuff, kids!" the beverage truck guy called. He started tossing bottles of Blu. Some of the girls, and some teenage boys who had been hanging out at the perimeter, turned to catch theirs, but at least half of the girls stuck tight to Trace as he made his way to an auto-graph table. It was ready with a chair, pens, a stack of bright blue drivers' cards, and Team Blu T-shirts.

"Can we have a picture?" one mom asked. Her daughter, cute and short, giggled.

"Sure," Harlan said. "Step right up, ladies."

Trace kept his sunglasses on, and the girl leaned in close and put her arm tight around him. The camera flashed—why, Trace was not sure, as it was bright sunlight.

"Thanks!" the girl said—then rushed off shrieking.

"Next," Harlan called.

Trace signed cards and T-shirts as fast as he could. The

line behind grew rather than shrank. He tried to say something, at least, to each kid. "Where'd you hear about Team
Blu?" he asked one mom-and-daughter combination.

"You're on TV," the mom said. She was a big, weathered blonde—a biker type with tattoos.

"We are?" Harlan said. He was right behind Trace.

"Yeah!" the daughter said. "The Blu ads are really
cool!"

"But your hair is shorter in them," the mom said, smiling at Trace. "I like it longer."

"Could you sign my arm?" the daughter asked.

"No body parts," Harlan said.

"I wish this was Sturgis," the mom said. "You could
sign my—"

"Next!" Harlan said.

Off to the side, Jimmy and Smoky (through a crack in
his window) kept an eye on the Super Stock—which drew
its own crowd. A bunch of men, clearly car guys, leaned
over the unbuttoned engine compartment, or into the
cockpit, or else knelt to look underneath the Super Stock.
Jimmy, in his company T-shirt, stood nearby; most of
them, Jimmy included, held a plastic bottle of Blu.

"Jimmy needs to get his license," Trace said to Harlan
as he signed the next card.

"He told you that?"

"Yup," Trace said. "Hey, thanks for coming today!"

"That boy ain't right," Harlan said softly. "Something
missing inside him. I don't know what it is, either."

"Could you sign my—"

"No body parts!" Harlan said. "Maybe it was his mother. She was wild. Died when he was only ten years old."

After a couple more young girls, the next one to step up to Trace's table was a brown-eyed cutie, dark-haired and about thirteen. "Hi there," Trace said.

She blushed, which made her even prettier.

"You're going to be really beautiful," Trace said to the girl as he scribbled his name.

"She already is!" her mother said from right behind the girl; she grabbed her daughter's elbow and marched her away from Trace.

"Mother!" the girl screeched, and they walked off jawing at each other.

"Nice move, kid," Harlan said as Trace signed the next T-shirt.

"Sorry. It just slipped out. Hey—thanks for coming today!" Trace said. He signed the next T-shirt.

Harlan said, "Car crash. That's how she died."

After the promo event, they saddled up and drove out to Gillette's Thunder Speedway just to look around.

"If you go off the track, you're certainly not going to hit any trees," Harlan said as he stepped out. He lit a cigarette. Beyond the empty speedway was open butte country; a power line's skinny towers shrank away, each one smaller, until the drooping lines disappeared in the plains. A couple of buzzards wheeled slow circles high overhead.

"Hey, the World of Outlaws sprint cars stop here," Jimmy said.

"Man, I'll bet they pack in the cowboys," Trace said, with a glance at Jimmy.

"We should race here, Pops!" Jimmy said.

"Nooooo way!" Harlan said, and faked a giant shiver.

"What is it about cowboys?" Jimmy asked.

"Not sure," Harlan said, taking a deep drag. "You're afraid of clowns, I'm afraid of cowboys. Maybe it's the hats."

After Gillette, Harlan pointed them straight west, toward the front range of the Bighorn Mountains. Trace rode up in the cab to get a better look at the rising landscape.

"You ain't ever seen mountains before?" Harlan asked Trace.

"Sure. I've been out West a couple of times with my old man, hunting."

"Hunting what?"

"Elk."

"Ever get one?"

"No."

"That's good," Harlan said.

"Good?" Trace said.

"Those big wide horns, and the way they stand around

in the water eating lily pads—it would be like shooting a duck on a pond," Harlan said.

"That would be a moose you're talking about," Trace said.

Jimmy, stretched out behind in the sleeper, snickered.

"Elk, moose," Harlan said.

"They're sort of similar. They both have antlers—not horns," Trace said.

"Antlers, horns," Harlan said, and shrugged.

"There's a difference," Trace said. "Antlers fall off every year, horns don't."

"If you know that kind of stuff, you've had plenty enough school," Harlan said.

"Which reminds me: we have to stop at the public library in Sheridan," Trace said.

"What?" Harlan replied, turning to Trace.

"Keep it on the road, Pops," Jimmy said.

Trace explained it in general terms. "It's like an assignment," he finished.

"Where in Sheridan is this library?" Harlan said.

"Right downtown, I think."

"Downtown? Where we gonna park this rig?" Jimmy asked.

Harlan squinted ahead toward the mountains. "I can park this baby between the coffee and the cream. It's libraries that scare me."

"And cowboys," Jimmy said.

After Buffalo, Wyoming, the Freightliner diesel and the Allison transmission buckled down through the rock and roll of U.S. 90. The land pitched upward, and Trace leaned forward in the cab to get a better view.

"You should see the Blue Ridge Mountains," Harlan said. "Not as tall and sharp, but prettier in my mind." He stared at the rising hills ahead. "This country makes me homesick."

The public library was near the intersection with Main Street. Harlan docked the big blue hauler right out front and put the flashers on. Like most truckers, he let the diesel idle.

"Coming in?" Trace asked.

"No way," Harlan said.

"Come on—it won't hurt you."

"I'll go," Jimmy said, surprising both Harlan and Trace.

"See?" Trace said. "Jimmy's not afraid."

"Okay," Harlan said. He looked in the mirror, adjusted his red bandanna, then followed Trace and Jimmy.

The library's reference desk was staffed by an outdoorsy-looking middle-aged woman with a reddish ponytail streaked with gray hair.

"Can I help you?" she said. Her eyes went from Trace and Jimmy to Harlan, who still wore his sunglasses.

Trace explained his assignment, which made the woman smile. Her name tag read JUDY.

"Well, I like your online teacher for sure," she said. It didn't take her long to show Trace the computerized catalog. "We might not have any books for you here, but certainly we can find some articles on microfiche."

"I'll look for books first," Trace said.

She left him alone, and Trace clicked through the screens. Sometime later, he looked around; the librarian was showing Harlan the magazine and newspaper section. Then she pointed to the blue rig outside the windows. Harlan nodded. They stood there talking. They were still talking several minutes later, when Trace headed across the library toward them.

"I've never met a real crew chief," the woman said.

"I'll bet not," Harlan said softly.

"You don't have to whisper," the librarian said to Harlan.

"I don't?" Harlan whispered.

Trace paused and pretended to look at a book on the shelf; he hated to ruin the magic.

"When's the last time you've been in a library?" she asked Harlan.

"Been a while," Harlan said, his voice cracking just above a whisper.

"Some men are afraid of librarians," the woman said. "I don't know why."

"I never met a librarian like you," Harlan said, his big neck starting to color.

The woman blushed, too.

Trace cleared his throat. "Excuse me," he said to her. "Could I get some help with the microfiche?"

An hour later, as they pulled away from the library, Harlan gave a toot from the air horn. The librarian stood on the front steps and gave a wave.

"Who-ee!" Harlan said. "I wished I lived in Sheridan."

"No you don't," Trace and Jimmy said at the same time.

"Or within striking distance, anyway," Harlan said, glancing in the side mirror.

"I've got her name and phone number," Trace said.

"Are you serious?" Harlan asked.

"Part of my assignment. Had to prove that I stopped," Trace said.

"I'll have to get that phone number from you sometime," Harlan said, faking a yawn.

"What's it worth to you?" Trace said. He flashed Judy's business card in front of Harlan's sunglasses.

Harlan snatched at it. "Give me that!"

"No way," Trace said.

"Keep it on the road, Pops!" Jimmy said.

The Billings Motorsports Park speedway lay several miles north of the city, toward Roundup. "It's fast and it's dirt!" was the BMP motto, and, as speedways went, it was better than many. To the north were buttes and open plains, but close in, early-bird fans had already spread out their blankets and stadium seats here and there on the sturdy aluminum bleachers. To the side, the pits were alive with race teams setting up. Harlan joined the lineup of haulers at the pit gate, and slowly crept ahead with the Team Blu rig. He kept looking in his side mirror.

"What?" Jimmy asked.

"Take a look behind," Harlan said.

Only a few haulers back was the open trailer with the orange No. 77x of Jason Nelson.

"He's everywhere," Trace muttered.

"I thought that kid was from Nebraska," Harlan said.

"He is," Trace said.

"What's he doing way up here?"

"Points?" Jimmy said, craning his neck to look.

"Billings is a long haul from Nebraska," Harlan said.

Trace was silent. When they finally reached the pit shack, the team got out and stepped up to the counter for the computer draw. Trace touched the mouse: number 97.

"Could be worse," said the cheerful girl at the pit shack computer.

"Yeah—like 100," said another girl. The two of them laughed.

"Thanks a lot," Harlan muttered as he paid for four pit passes.

"Four?" the first girl asked, looking behind as she laid out wristbands.

"That guy in the little motor home—he's with us, too," Harlan said.

"Two vehicles will cost extra," the girl said.

"No problem," Harlan said.

"Couldn't do without your motor guy, eh?" said someone behind in line. It was Jason Nelson's father.

Harlan gave him a long stare, but said nothing.

Beside his father, Jason lifted his chin at Trace. "Hey, man."

Trace nodded back.

"Swap motors tonight?" Jason's father asked Team Blu. "Just for the hell of it?"

Harlan spit to the side. "Ignore those farmers," he muttered.

"Here you boys go," the pit shack girls said.

Trace, Jimmy, and Harlan held out their arms; the girls looped their wrists with colored bands and sealed them.

"What about his?" the younger girl said, glancing toward Smoky's motor home. She held the fourth wristband.

"He's kind of . . . handicapped," Harlan said. "He'll drive up and put his arm out the window. Could you do his wristband?"

"Sure," the girl said.

Harlan pulled the Freightliner up far enough to let Smoky stop his mini–motor home by the shack. Then he, Jimmy, and Trace hung out Harlan's window to watch. As the shack girl came forward with Smoky's wristband, Smoky held out his arm. The pit shack girl flinched— nearly tripped—at the sight of his claw-fingered hand.

"Yes!" Jimmy said, and pumped his fist.

"We are sick, sick puppies," Harlan said as he geared the hauler forward.

Smoky followed close behind, like a little dog following a big dog, and parked alongside the big hauler. Soon the rear door came up, and Jimmy and Harlan rolled out

the Super Stock. The early appearance of the Blu car surprised Trace.

"Are we ready to race?" he asked Smoky.

"We're always ready to race," Smoky rasped.

Trace glanced up toward the roof of Smoky's motor
home. The little satellite dish was not erect.

Trace started last in the third heat. The track was hot,
black, and dry. "I swear it's got coal in it," Jimmy had said
earlier, holding up a handful of dark dirt for Harlan's
inspection. But Trace got good bite out of the corners, and
he finished third of eight cars.

"Looking good," Harlan called as Trace rumbled up to
the hauler. From habit, Trace braked before the loading
ramps and killed the engine. "Setup is on the money," he
said, tossing his helmet to Harlan, "but the top end felt
doggy."

"Smoky says we're good," Harlan said. "Fresh rubber is
all we need."

Trace glanced inside the trailer at Smoky, who looked
off toward the track.

In the feature, Trace started in the fifth row, outside—
about the middle of the pack. Jason Nelson sat third row
inside. Trace worked his butt off, high and low, to move up
several slots, but some of the local cars were not set up
right, resulting in spinouts and yellow flag after yellow
flag. It was a race with no rhythm or flow.

On the fourth restart, single file, Trace powered up in

sixth place, with Jason Nelson in third. Due to wrecks and mechanical problems, the field of Super Stocks was significantly down—Trace could count only a dozen cars. In any race there was always a moment, a window of opportunity. With ten laps remaining and the cars starting to string out, he found a high line and got ready to take names and kick butts. He mashed the pedal to the floor, but something was missing. He couldn't pull by anyone, least of all Jason Nelson. There was just enough motor to get him into third place, where he hung on as the laps counted down. Nelson caught a break on the last yellow flag; the car in front of him spun out, which put Nelson in second place for the restart. Yellow flags closed up the field, and Nelson managed to get his nose inside yellow No. 27, a local car, on the green flag. The two of them banged away at each other for the final laps, with Nelson winning by a car length. The end of the race was a crowd-pleaser, with Trace finishing a close third.

Coming off the scales, he paused alongside Nelson and gunned the engine. Nelson nodded back—and grinned like a fool. Trace spun up dust and headed to the pits.

Jimmy was waiting by the hauler with the cable; Smoky was nowhere to be seen.

"Good going!" Harlan said as Trace pulled himself from the cockpit. "Third place every night would win a season's points chase."

Trace wiped sweat from his forehead. "If I had the motor we had in Huron, we'd have a checkered flag."

"I'll have Smoky look at it," Harlan said.

"I told you after the heat race that it was doggy," Trace said, and kicked dirt.

"Don't get your shorts in a wad," Harlan said. "I'm happy with third."

"I'm not," Trace said.

"That's what I like to hear!" Harlan said.

"Next time you'll have all the motor you need," Smoky said to Trace. His gravelly voice came through the screened window of his motor home. "If we win every night, people will think we're cheating."

Harlan and Jimmy laughed like that was the funniest thing in the world.

8

Team Blu convoyed east across North Dakota, heading for Fargo and the Friday night races at Red River Valley Speedway. On the way, they did promo stops in Bismarck and Jamestown; the crowds were bigger each time. In Jamestown, Trace signed T-shirts and leaned in for pictures as three Blu beverage guys handed out free stuff.

"It's the power of television," Harlan remarked as Trace worked to shorten up the never-ending line.

"Nothing to do with me?" Trace asked, scribbling his name on another driver card. After an hour, his signature had turned into a chicken scratch, but nobody seemed to mind.

"Nope," Harlan said. "With TV ads and free stuff, we could put Jimmy in the car and still draw a crowd."

"Thanks a lot," Trace said.

"Yeah, thanks, Pops!" Jimmy called from over by the car.

At this point in the afternoon, they didn't care what people heard them say. The line moved forward like an assembly line; Trace scrawled his name like a factory worker ratcheting down the same nut again and again. He signed for two full hours, making sure to get to everyone, after which he dragged himself inside the trailer. His wrist hurt.

"I think we've gone viral," Jimmy said.

Trace headed up to his cabin and took a shower. He let the hot water run over him until it turned cool, but as he toweled off he still felt greasy. Gritty. Something. Signing autographs was like a sugar high—fun at the moment, but afterward it left him feeling edgy and empty. He was happy when the big diesel engine rattled alive and the hauler began to move. He flopped onto his bed, closed his eyes, and counted the Allison nine-speed gear shifts. When they were rolling down the highway, he always slept like a baby, but never until Harlan reached freeway speed. It had something to do with the silky flow of the transmission, the rocking motion of the trailer . . .

He woke up much later to silence. It was very early morning, and they were parked at a rest stop somewhere in the middle of North Dakota. He got up, pulled on a sweatshirt. The trailer was quiet below. He stepped outside into low, pink sunlight and the fresh, wet scent of prairie. It had rained during the night; flat spring wheat fields stretched far away south. Closer in, a black-and-white magpie fluttered in the thin grove of trees; a blue jay sat perched on a Dumpster, looking expectantly at Trace for a handout.

He was stiff from sleeping, and took a walk to stretch his legs. Behind the rest stop was a shallow drainage ditch with a narrow ridge on the other side. He leaped across, then began to walk along the field. The weeds and grass were silvery with dew. A hen pheasant flushed—startling him—and he paused to watch it flutter and glide, flutter and glide, to where it touched down in a patch of tall grass. He swung his own arms wide to loosen his shoulder muscles, and breathed deeply. If he closed his eyes, it felt like he was ten years old, and back on the farm. He walked on, glancing occasionally behind at the silent, shiny blue hauler—if its engine fired up, he would have to hustle back—but the only sounds were the intermittent whir of freeway traffic, and the sudden call of a meadowlark. That was a sound from when he was kid; meadowlarks were mostly gone from Minnesota, and he walked carefully forward until he saw it, perched on the stub of an ancient gray fence post. The bird had a yellow throat with a black tie. It sang and sang; no other meadowlark answered.

At that moment a door clacked back by the hauler. Trace turned. Harlan walked to Smoky's motor home and rapped sharply on the slide-out; Smoky handed out a pack of cigarettes. Trace took a last look at the meadowlark and the glistening blue-green fields, then turned back.

After a short walk he came across the ditch and through the trees—just as Harlan headed toward the men's john.

"Boo!"

"Jesus!" Harlan shouted, and jumped sideways. "Don't scare me like that."

"Sorry," Trace said.

"Where you been?" Harlan said. His eyes went to the wet cuffs of Trace's jeans.

"Took a little walk," Trace said, nodding over his shoulder toward the prairie.

"Don't do that, either," Harlan said. "You might get lost."

They pulled into West Fargo on Thursday evening, and ate at the Speedway Restaurant on Main Avenue West.

"Anybody from Minnesota coming over to the races tomorrow night?" Harlan asked.

"My dad, I think," Trace said, glancing at his phone text messages, which kept coming. "Some of my friends, maybe."

"You better make sure," Harlan said. "Don't want to get your fence bunnies mixed up."

"I don't have any fence bunnies," Trace shot back.

"At least not like Smoky, back in the day," Harlan said.

Smoky shrugged. "I had my fun. Glad I did, as it turned out."

They fell silent. Harlan shrugged. "Hey, you never know," he said.

During dinner Jimmy and Smoky went around and around about the rear-end setup. The Red River track was a half-mile oval—most speedways were a quarter or a third mile—which required a different gear ratio. The lower the ratio, the better the power out of the corners. But lower gearing was a drag on the top-end speed down the straightaways—plus it forced the engine to run at higher rpm.

"What do *you* like?" Harlan asked Trace.

"Thought you'd never ask," Trace replied.

"Sorry," Jimmy said. It was like he and Smoky suddenly remembered they had a driver—and not just a car.

"I like torque, and I like speed," Trace said. "But if I have to choose, I'll take torque any day."

"Exactly," Jimmy said, with a grin for Smoky.

"Okay," Smoky said. "But by the time you hit the corners, you're going to be red-lining."

"Your motors can handle it," Harlan said.

"We're running a 360 Chevy," Smoky muttered, "not an Indy car."

"That's why Laura pays you the big money," Harlan said.

"Right," Smoky said.

Their waitress came to inquire about dessert; she didn't look twice at Smoky, which got her a big tip.

As they walked out of the restaurant, Trace said to Harlan, "You mind if I disappear for a while?"

"With who, and what's 'a while'?"

"A local driver I know."

Harlan shrugged. "Sure. Why not? It's good to have buddies. It's not like you need to hang out with us 24-7."

"Thanks, Dad," Trace said.

"Mind if Jimmy goes along?" Harlan asked.

Trace hesitated.

"I can't—I've got stuff to do," Jimmy said quickly.

At that moment, Sara Bishop drove up fast in a 1970 Chevelle, silver with black rally stripes.

"What the—?" Harlan began, ready to leap to safety.

"Don't worry, I'll have him back before ten!" Sara called to Team Blu.

Trace jumped inside, and Sara smoked the tires in first gear as they left.

"Just had to do that," she said.

"Great ride!" Trace said, looking around the Chevy. It had a bench seat, original four-speed shifter, round gauges—all of it stock.

"My dad's," she said. "I get to drive it once a month. I saved it up for tonight." At the first stoplight, she leaned over for a hug. She smelled girly and fresh—not like rubber and race fuel—and her hair was longer. "Hey, Mr. Television Star," she said.

He had forgotten what a cute mouth she had. "At least I'm not selling dog food," Trace said.

"Or used cars," she said.

"Or laxatives."

"Or panty liners," she said.

She was easy to be with, and Trace relaxed as they cruised toward Fargo.

"Where do you want to go?" she asked.

"Anywhere," Trace said.

As she braked for a stoplight, a late-model Mustang, all paint and no engine, pulled close alongside. The driver was a comb-over artist who had watched too many Elvis movies. He kept staring at Sara and her Chevelle.

"Okay, okay," she said, glancing his way; she brought up the rpm. Adding a half clutch and lot of brake, she hunched up the Chevelle's rear end. The Mustang guy did the same. At green, Sara hole-shot him big-time—several car lengths with a lot of blue smoke—then let him go. She laughed as he raced on by himself.

"That was mean," Trace said.

"That was fun," she said, turning north into a neighborhood. "Want to see our shop?"

Fargo was short on trees, but Sara's parents' home had two big elms in the backyard and a metal-sided shop tucked between them. They parked in the alley; she unlocked a side door, and they went inside.

"Wow!" Trace said. The shop was bright, immaculate, and totally filled with old-school memorabilia: gas pumps with the glass jars on top, old filling station signs, skinny tires on the wall, even displays of original quarts of oil in paper cans with tin tops.

"My dad's a collector," she said. "He and my mom

travel all over on weekends, looking for gas station stuff."

In contrast to the automotive antiques, the Bishop Super Stock looked like a battered spaceship from another planet. Trace walked over to it. "Are you racing tomorrow night?"

Sara followed him, and touched the roof of the Super Stock. " 'Fraid not. We don't have enough motor for the half mile," she said. "I do best on short tracks, like Grand Forks and Buffalo River."

"But you're coming?"

"Wouldn't miss it," she said. They were standing close now.

Their eyes met for a long moment; he could not stop himself from reaching out and touching her hair.

She closed her eyes but didn't pull away. "How's Mel?" she asked.

He traced a finger around her ear, then touched her lips. "She's . . . busy. The racetrack, school."

"Amber told me about prom," Sara said, opening her eyes. They were alive and shiny. "You really screwed that up."

"Yes. For sure!" Trace said. He pulled back his hand and leaned against her car. "I don't know what I was thinking."

She stepped close in front of him. "If there's ever a line that a girl likes to hear, it's that one."

"Which one?"

" 'I don't know what I was thinking.' "

Trace looped his arms around her waist. They were

back to one of those in-between moments: friends or a whole lot more.

"I bet I know a boy's favorite line to hear," she murmured.

"What would that be?" Trace asked.

" 'I'm not busy at all tonight.' "

He pulled her sharply forward and kissed her. She felt nothing at all like Mel, but if he closed his eyes . . .

"Mmmmm," she breathed, and pressed back even harder. She was hard-bodied, like a gymnast, a dancer.

"What about your parents?" Trace said.

"They're up in Rolla at some auction," she said. "My brother—he's fourteen—ditched me to stay overnight with a friend. So it's just me."

"Whoa," Trace breathed.

" 'Whoa' like with horses, when they're supposed to stop?" she asked. "Or more like 'Whoa, I can't believe my good luck?' "

Trace kissed her again.

Sara dropped him off at two a.m. beside the silent hauler in the shadowy parking lot. He didn't get out immediately. They sat in silence.

"I know that you really love Mel," she said. "So this was . . . nothing, all right?"

Trace didn't know what to say. He touched her hair again.

She looked through the windshield toward the dark back of the speedway bleachers.

"It's true. But tonight was not 'nothing,' " Trace said.

When she turned back to him, her eyes glistened with tears.

"What?" Trace asked.

"I finally meet a guy I can talk with, and who seems to think I'm pretty—but he's taken."

"Please," Trace began.

"Don't lie to me about Mel," Sara said. "I'll only feel worse."

At the pit entrance to the Red River Valley Speedway, a guy in a green safety vest came alongside. "Are you together?" he asked, glancing behind at Smoky's motor home.

"That's right," Harlan said.

"Only one hauler per race car in the pits," the man said.

"If there's an extra fee, we'll pay," Harlan said.

"Sorry. Read our rule book," the guy said. "We try to give our fans an unobstructed view."

"Hang on a second," Harlan said. He climbed out and went back to Smoky's motor home. In the mirror, Trace watched them; Smoky gestured once, then twice. Harlan shrugged, then nodded.

"We're gonna drop off the car," he said, "then take the motor home into the pits."

"That'll work. Park your tall hauler over in the Schatz

Lot," the guy said, and pointed. Then he waved them forward.

"Why we doing it that way?" Jimmy asked. "I need my stuff."

"Smoky wants it that way," Harlan said.

"I thought you were the crew chief," Jimmy muttered.

Red River had a prerace inspection lane, which was always the sign of a top-notch speedway. Jimmy and Harlan rolled the Blu Super Stock forward, then waited while the tech guys measured the car: tip of the nose spoiler to the front wheel hub, overall wheelbase, roof height, height of the deck lid in relation to the rear quarter panel, and more—anything that had to do with airflow.

Trace and Harlan watched. "Back in the day, Smoky once built a car to 15/16 scale," Harlan said. "It kept beating everybody. Cut through the air like a bird. The track officials tore it apart after every race, but they could never find anything wrong. He finally got caught when another car came up and parked alongside him. You could tell that Smoky's car was way smaller."

"Okay, Blu, you're good to go," the tech guy called. "See you after the races—especially if you win."

Harlan gave him a look. "You say that to everybody?"

"Yup," the man said.

The stands began to fill well before the time trials. Trace took a call from his father. "We were going to get pit passes," he said, "but then Linda thought we could see better from the stands." His voice was overly cheerful, and Linda giggled in the background.

You mean, they serve alcohol in the stands but not in the pits?
"Okay, no problem," Trace said.

"So we'll see you after the races, right?"

"Later," Trace said.

Harlan looked at him. "That sounded like bad news."

"No, good news, actually," he said, and left it at that. With some time on his hands, he wandered down pit row to look at the Late Models and the sprint cars. A Late Model looked much like a Super Stock but had a slightly shorter front end, plus a rear spoiler. The spoiler, tilted up to create downforce on the rear tires, was the giveaway—that, and the sweet smell of the methanol fuel they used. New Late Model engines out of the crate cost as much as brand-new, turn-key Super Stocks.

But in racing, there was always another level. A Late Model was a kiddie car compared with a sprint, where the top class had a 410-cubic-inch, 700-horsepower motor driving a much lighter car on a much shorter wheelbase. The main thing that kept a sprint car from lifting off the track like a fighter jet was the big downdraft wing on top—that and the two rear tires, which were as wide and fat as state fair hogs. It took guts to drive a sprint car.

Trace paused beside a local sprint car team sponsored by Moffett Farms, who were potato growers near Fargo. The pit crew ignored Trace, who was not yet in his racing suit. The No. 82 car was clean and new, but the team had a vibe of new money and not enough experience. Trace walked on. The big sponsors—Pennzoil, National Guard,

Snap-on tools, Quaker State, and others—were not here tonight. Instead it was all teams with regional sponsors: cement contractors, heavy-equipment rentals, beer distributors, and potato growers.

"How ya doing, kid?" said an older fellow by a battered sprint car.

"Good," Trace said.

"Want to look at the car?"

"Sure," Trace said.

"We can use all the fans we can get," he said, and gave Trace a walkaround. The red sprint car's tires were worn, its wing had a serious wrinkle, and the dented but freshly painted sides were covered in smaller decals, all local sponsors; they ranged from an insurance agent to a whole foods store.

"My daughter's place," the man said of the whole foods decal. "It's on Broadway, downtown Fargo. She can't afford to pay anything, but she packs us lunch for the races. You should stop there."

"You must eat healthy," Trace said.

"I sneak off and eat speedway chicken, myself," the man said. His eyes returned to the car. "But we get by," he said. "And that's the good thing about a mostly independent car like ours—it puts the focus back on the driver. Anybody can win if you've got an unlimited budget."

Trace was silent. Then he said, "Who's your driver?"

"My son," the man said proudly. "He's thirty now. Been racing since he was hardly big enough to fit into a go-kart.

Doing great. One of these years, somebody's going to take notice and give him a real ride."

"Good luck tonight," Trace said, and walked on. A couple of rows over was the orange Super Stock of Jason Nelson; Trace thought of walking past, but didn't.

Back in the central pit area, Team Blu—except for Smoky—sat in lawn chairs underneath the awning of Smoky's Gulf Stream. A stack of fresh tires, a floor jack, a generator, and Jimmy's giant toolbox on wheels sat beside the blue Super Stock.

"All we need is a barbecue kettle and some weenies, and we'd be back to Flintstone Speedway—where you came from," Harlan said as Trace approached.

"Nothing wrong with that," Trace said.

"Makes me nervous," Jimmy said; he meant being away from the big hauler.

"I told you: if we need some work done between heats and the feature, Trace drives back to the hauler," Harlan said.

"Still . . ." Jimmy said, and trailed off.

"You boys worry too much," Smoky said from behind his window screen. From inside the Gulf Stream came the sounds of NASCAR on television. Smoky's satellite dish was cupped to the sky.

Time trials were another sign of a professional speedway. Each car took two fast laps, with the best time used for heat race placement. On his first lap Trace got squirrelly in turn 2, but on his second lap he hit his marks and knocked off a full three seconds.

"That first lap was me—my fault—don't change a thing!" Trace said as he came into the pits.

"That's what we like to hear," Harlan said.

Super Stocks ran second of four classes, right after Street Stocks and before Late Models; Trace's time trials numbers put him in the second row, inside, for the heat race. Jason Nelson—who else?—lined up two rows back.

On the second lap the lead Super Stock threw a right front tire—pitching the car sideways, where he was T-boned by the following car. Both left for the pits and could not make the three-slow-laps window to return. That put Trace in second place. He had good power—not great, but enough to gradually reel in the lead car and complete the pass on the eighth lap. From then on it was a question of hitting his spots in the corners. He avoided mistakes, and took the checkered flag by two car lengths.

Back in the pits, Harlan and Jimmy each pretended to be reading a newspaper as Trace rumbled in. Except that they held the newspapers upside down.

"Very funny!" Trace said as he killed the motor.

Harlan caught his helmet, and Jimmy almost tipped his chair over, laughing. "That's the way to do it!" Harlan said.

Smoky was actually outside, in daylight, though he wore long sleeves, gloves, and a wide, floppy fishing hat for maximum sun protection.

"Motor feel all right?" he rasped.

"Decent," Trace said, exiting backward from the cock-pit, "but no real sweet spot."

Smoky nodded to Jimmy, who quickly hooked up the hauler cable. As Jimmy stood uncertainly by the car, Smoky said to Trace, "Would you go over to the food shack and get me a cola?" He fished a twenty-dollar bill from his shirt pocket.

"Why don't you go with him, Jimmy?" Harlan said. "Trace might run into those cowboys from Nebraska and need some muscle."

"Sure," Jimmy said.

"Yeah, what do we know about engines?" Trace added.

When Trace and Jimmy returned, Smoky was all done working on the car.

In the feature, Trace ended up in the pole position—his least favorite starting slot. The inside, first-row spot was overrated. All the pressure was on the lead driver; there was no car ahead to draft or to learn from. A good part of racing strategy was watching the cars in front—how they handled the turns, where they rocked and rolled over a hole or a soft spot. Having the pole position was like being point man on a combat patrol: get out there and draw fire while everybody else hangs back.

After leading for three laps, Trace got overly aggressive and missed his spot in turn 4—doing a loop-de-loop right in front of the grandstand. The worst part was hearing the cheers as he was waved to the rear for the restart. There were very few times on the racetrack when anger was helpful, but this was one of them. Starting in the rear after beginning in the pole position was a driver's ultimate humiliation; Trace fixed his eyes on the lead car—red No. 47, already a half lap ahead at the green flag—and stepped down hard with his right foot.

He made up two or three spots quickly, then ground it out through the middle laps. As the laps counted down on the scoreboard, his car got faster and faster; it wasn't like down in South Dakota, where his engine surged. This time it grew in rpm, slowly, lap by lap. With more engine, he had a better feel for the track, for the suspension, for the turns; as with riding a bicycle or planing across a lake on water skis, the more speed, the sharper the turns. With huge torque out of the corners, and red-line rpm down the stretch, he began to eat up cars like an alligator swimming behind a line of ducks.

By lap 17 of the twenty-lap feature, he was in fourth place. Jason Nelson, in third, tried to block him right and left, but Trace had too much car for Nelson and got by him. Some races belong to a driver from lap 1, and Trace felt ashamed that he had—even briefly—let go of that feeling.

He kept playing the lead two cars, probing for daylight. When he found a crack, he slipped between and challenged them three-wide. The triplicate of Super Stocks roared deep into turn 4, drifting sideways like three fish in the same school, but it was Trace who nosed stronger out of the turn. The other two tucked in behind him, and Trace surged the last two laps to take the checkered.

He pounded the wheel and pumped his fist all the way to the scale. After a moment on the scale, he was waved toward the winner's circle for a quick photo. Emerging from the car, he waved to the crowd. Sara—he was sure it was her—jumped up and down and waved. There was cheering, but more than a few boos and jeers.

"You and Kasey Kahne," the trophy girl said as she leaned against Trace for the photo. "People love to hate you."

"I'm a tough guy," Trace said.

"You sure look like one," she murmured. "I love those Blu TV ads—how you get in and out of the car—but you really need a chick in them."

"Like who?" Trace said, keeping his smile fixed for the cameras. There was some commotion in the stands, but Trace could not see well after the flash from the camera.

"Like me, sweetheart," the girl said. She kept her face toward the camera.

Then it was off to tech lane.

"Nice work, kid!" Harlan shouted as Trace pulled in behind the other top-four finishers.

Jimmy hustled over to spray the radiator, aiming his hose and disappearing in a hissing cloud of steam.

"Don't thank me!" Trace said, watching the temp slowly fall. "I was red-lining every lap. I can't believe this motor!"

"Neither can a lot of people," said Jason Nelson's father. He was standing just ahead, by Jason, who had finished fourth.

"Maybe it's your driver—ever thought of that?" Harlan threw back.

The older Nelson swore and came forward.

A tech guy in a green safety vest hustled over. "Please stay with your car," he said to Nelson. Then he turned to Trace. "Please drive forward to the tech shack."

"What did I tell you?" the older Nelson said.

Harlan ignored him, and followed Trace forward.

Inside the tech shack, the crew was quick and efficient; two guys worked on the top end, while another pair worked underneath the car, dropping the oil pan in order to get a look at the crankshaft. Within twenty minutes they were done.

"Have a nice day," the lead tech guy said, like a cop after a traffic stop.

"You can bet on it," Harlan said.

Jimmy put the oil pan back on to keep out the dust (they would need fresh oil and a new pan gasket), after which a speedway ATV bumped up behind, and pushed the Blu car back toward their pit slot.

Steering the silent Super Stock down pit row, Trace kept his eyes forward. In his peripheral vision, he saw other drivers and their crews turn to look. And it was Trace's forward focus that made him see it: Smoky's Gulf Stream, and the satellite dish on top. It was pointed not skyward but toward the track.

Worse, waiting by the little motor home was Laura Williams, Team Blu's big boss; Carlos, the photographer; and Tasha.

"We've got visitors," called Harlan, who had caught a ride on the back of the ATV. "Didn't tell you earlier because I didn't want to make you nervous."

"Thanks a lot," Trace muttered.

Laura was dressed in her usual power business suit—black short skirt and pale silk blouse—with her signature flaming red lipstick. Carlos had his artsy look going, with tight black pants and a lime-green Hawaiian shirt; a big digital camera covered his face as he snapped away.

"Did we pass inspection?" Laura asked. She was not big on greetings.

"Always do," Harlan said with a big smile.

"What was that all about over in the stands?" Laura said. She was not smiling.

"You mean, fans not happy that we won?" Harlan asked.

"Yes," Laura said. "And there was a fight of some kind. I didn't like that booing, that 'checkered flag cheater' stuff."

"Redneck locals," Harlan said dismissively. "Like I told Tasha down in South Dakota—people root for the home-town boys."

"But why would so many of them not like us?" Laura asked.

"Because we're winning," Harlan boomed. He threw a beefy arm around Trace. "People hate winners, and we're winners because Team Blu has the real deal for a driver—did you see him come from last to first?"

"Yes. Pretty swift," Laura said. "Literally."

"Glad you caught the race," Trace said, unzipping his suit partway as he wiped his sweaty, dusty face. "Didn't know you were coming."

"Hold that!" Carlos called.

"We like to check up on our people from time to time," Laura said to Trace. "Especially since we missed you down in Iowa."

"Trace and I had our talk," Tasha said.

Laura pursed her narrow, bright lips. "Actually, we all need to have a little talk—a team meeting," she said.

"Uh-oh," Harlan said, trying to make a joke.

"Now?" Laura asked, turning to Tasha.

"Why not?" Tasha said.

"Somewhere out of the dust?" Laura said as a car on an open trailer rumbled by. She waved dust away from her pale face.

"Let's meet back at the office," Harlan said, nodding across toward the Blu hauler.

"Uh, Laura?" Carlos interrupted. "Can I shoot Trace outside while he's still sweaty?"

"Sure," Laura said.

"I need a bunch of new shots by the car," Carlos said, taking Trace's arm and steering him into position. "The light is fabulous right now—still some sun, but the overhead track lights are working great as fill-in."

Tasha and the others watched.

"Can you unzip your suit a little more?" Carlos asked as he fired away.

Expressionless, Trace obeyed. Tasha looked away.

"Your hair's getting long," Carlos said with a pained look. "You're starting to look Italian playboy."

"I noticed that, too," Laura said.

"I told him he was looking like a hippie," Harlan said.

"You thrash the car, I'll worry about my hair," Trace muttered.

"No, *we'll* worry about your hair," Laura countered.

Trace set his jaw and said nothing.

"Fabulous—love the angry look!" Carlos exclaimed. "Hold please!"

Laura turned to Tasha. "Be sure to find Trace a good stylist before our next photo shoot."

"Sure," Tasha said flatly.

They headed back to the Freightliner, where Jimmy quickly clattered together some chairs. Team Blu, with Laura and Tasha, and Carlos shooting away, assembled inside the brightly lit trailer.

"I'm here with good news," Laura said.

"Better than winning a feature?" Harlan said, with a nudge to Jimmy.

"Yes, actually," Laura said. "You might have noticed some 'movement,' we'll call it, in your promo appearances?"

"No kidding," Jimmy said.

"That's because our Blu ad campaign has been successful beyond anyone's expectations," Laura said.

"Yahoo!" Jimmy said.

"Pipe down," Harlan whispered.

"In the corporate and financial world, there's always a *but* that follows good news," Laura continued. "But in our case"—she laughed at her own joke—"there is none. In its first three months, Blu energy drink has achieved a five percent share of the national energy drink market."

"Is that good?" Harlan asked.

"It means that Red Bull and all the other drinks had better be looking over their shoulders," Laura said.

Jimmy and Harlan high-fived.

Laura went on. "Our marketing strategy of authenticity, grassroots, heartland appeal—"

"And a very hot driver," Carlos added as he fired away.

"Yes, that, too," Laura said, stepping over to fluff up Trace's sweaty hair. "All of it has been on the money in every way. In the big world of Karchers and Ladwin Agribusiness, Blu energy drink is a rising star. And everybody at headquarters loves Team Blu."

There was silence in the trailer. Laura looked at the group with a smile, and kept her hand on Trace's shoulder. He stared across the trailer without expression.

"Somewhere there's gotta be a *but* or a *however*," Harlan said.

"We can't think of any," Tasha said. "Trace has even been taking care of his homework."

"So this means we can keep racing?" Jimmy asked, with a wink to Trace.

"Remember when we launched this program?" Laura said, looking down at Trace. "How I said that we didn't

need to win every race? That we just needed to compete?"

Trace nodded.

"Well, corporate has changed its mind. We like winning
—winning is fun," she said. She pushed back a lock of hair
from Trace's forehead.

"We like it, too," Harlan said. There were grins all
around—except for Trace.

"But to answer Jimmy's question: yes, Team Blu can
keep racing," Laura said. "In fact, our budget has been
increased. Assuming the rest of this year goes as well as it
is now, we have plans to expand Team Blu racing."

"Expand?" Harlan asked.

"How so?" Jimmy said quickly.

"We are considering moving you up to a more national
car class," Laura said.

Harlan looked puzzled.

"Such as Late Models or sprint cars," Laura said.

There was stunned silence in the trailer.

"Sprints?" Trace breathed. He got goose bumps on his
forearms.

"Yes. I prefer them over Late Models, actually," Laura
said. "Sprint cars offer a fan base that has more money to
spend—plus they have those pretty wings on top with all
that advertising space."

For once, Harlan and Jimmy were speechless.

"Unless you think you couldn't handle a sprint car,"
Laura said to Team Blu.

"You just watch us!" Harlan said.

Trace glanced at Tasha, then looked up at Laura. "This is for sure?"

Laura shrugged. "Nothing in business is for sure, but it's highly likely. We have a winning team and a winning product. The nature of business is to keep expanding—to get to the top."

"The top for me would be a Blu NASCAR ride," Harlan said. He was joking, as always.

"If we keeping winning and growing, in a couple of years that's not impossible," Laura said.

Jimmy rocked back in his chair as if hit by a Taser. His mouth hung open—and Harlan, too, was speechless.

Laura turned to Trace and smiled. "Any questions, Mr. Driver?"

Trace swallowed. "No. Not really. Just one for Tasha, but we can do that later."

Tasha gave him a quizzical look.

"Must be about his homework," Harlan said.

"You don't look all that happy," Laura said, tilting her head to look at Trace.

Trace was silent.

"That's his normal look," Harlan said. "Ice Man. That's what we should call him."

"I guess if you're a driver, that's a good thing," Laura said. She turned to the group. "We'll meet up later for dinner and celebrate this properly, all right?"

"Yahoo!" Jimmy crowed again.

After the meeting ended, Tasha hung around the trailer. Finally Harlan and Jimmy stepped outside.

"What?" Tasha asked. She kept her voice down.

Trace took a deep breath. "We're cheating," he said.

"Huh? What are you talking about?" Tasha asked.

"Our motor. Our team. We're winning because we're cheating."

"How do you know this?" she whispered.

"I can't prove it, but I'm nearly a hundred percent sure we are."

"How?" Tasha asked.

"It's a motor thing. It's complicated," Trace said.

Tasha swore briefly. She looked around the trailer. "I always wondered why we hired those Southern boys. There were plenty of car builders in the Midwest."

Trace was silent. Then he said, "So what do we do?"

Tasha gave him a long look. "Nothing right now."

Harlan poked his head back into the trailer. "Driver needed. Your fans are here!"

Trace stepped outside to clapping. A group of people—including Trace's father and his girlfriend, Linda—had clustered by the door. His father had a scuffed red cheek, a black-crusty nostril, plus some drops of blood on his 18x T-shirt.

"What happened to you?" Trace asked.

"There were these idiots in front of us," Linda said

quickly. She had high hair and a tight sweater. "They kept ragging on you and Team Blu. They were really drunk and—"

"And I asked them to lay off," Don Bonham said. "I said, 'Hey, that's my kid out there.' "

"It sort of went downhill from there," Linda said, and giggled.

"Don't tell me you got into a fight!" Trace said.

"Not really a fight fight," Linda began, and leaned closer to Trace—she was unsteady on her feet—which was when Harlan stepped up.

"Thanks, honey, for sticking up for Team Blu," he said, taking Linda by the elbow and steering her to the side, "but Trace has some people to see right now."

"Great race, Son," Don said, and gave Trace a clumsy hug.

Trace glanced at a cluster of parents waiting with their kids, boys and girls, who held Trace Bonham T-shirts. To the side was Sara Bishop; she was talking with Tasha. "Thanks," he said. "I gotta go."

Trace worked the crowd, pausing to watch his father and Linda walk away—then headed over to Sara and Tasha.

"You remember Sara?" Tasha asked.

"Sure," Trace said. "We've been in touch."

Sara blushed and looked away.

"Oh, God. Don't tell me," Tasha said.

Neither Sara nor Trace said anything.

"Anyway, I guess we're all friends here," Tasha said. "So I might as well tell you something. Sara was the runner-up for the Team Blu ride."

"I was?" Sara asked. She blinked rapidly.

"For sure," Tasha said. "You had that cute girl-in-a-man's-world thing going. The freckles, the mouth, the short hair. We liked you a lot."

"Thanks," Sara said flatly. "But all I got was this generic rejection letter."

"That's the corporate way—sorry," Tasha replied. "But you definitely were our second choice."

Sara looked sideways at the big, shiny Team Blu hauler. When she looked back to Trace, he knew something had changed—she was suddenly a step farther away from him. Receding. Then out of reach.

"Jason Nelson was our third choice," Tasha continued. "He has a lot to offer, too. It was a tough call for us, choosing among the three of you."

There was silence. "I should go," Sara said.

"Wait," Trace called, but Sara was already heading off.

"What are you trying to do?" Trace said to Tasha. In the harsh light of the parking lot, she looked like a stranger.

"Do?" Tasha said. "I'm only sharing information that I thought you'd like to know. We're all adults here, right?"

Trace was silent.

"And about that cheating thing," Tasha said, stepping closer. Her voice was low and flat. "I've thought about the whole thing, and it didn't take me long to decide. If I were you, I'd let it go. Business is based on facts. We race, we go through the tech inspections, we pass those inspections. Those are the facts."

"Yeah, but—"

"But nothing," she said, cutting him off. "Right now, the only one who says we're cheating is you."

Trace looked toward the track.

Tasha moved even closer. "Here's my deal," she said, lowering her voice further. "I've worked my ass off to get into advertising, and this Team Blu gig on my résumé is like having aces in a poker game. Same thing for you as a driver, I would think."

Trace met her gaze; her dark eyes were no longer sexy, but flat and cold.

"So until someone proves we're cheating, we're not cheating. And if you want to make a fuss about it, we've got other drivers who would be happy to take your ride."

9

Saturday night took Team Blu to Grand Forks, North Dakota, and Rivers Speedway, one of Trace's favorites. It was a tight, very high-banked quarter-mile track—and the site of the Team Blu tryouts last summer. Back then he had arrived with his father in their Chevy Tahoe and a dusty duffel bag full of racing gear. Now he rumbled down pit row in the cab of the big blue rig, past the World of Outlaws trailers.

"Look out, boys, here we come!" Harlan hollered at the national teams.

"We're not there yet," Trace said, but Harlan and Jimmy weren't listening. Their enthusiasm was hard to ignore; it made him forget about last night. Tonight, the

World of Outlaws sprint cars would put fifteen thousand fans in the stands. Trace had been coming to Rivers Speedway since he was a kid. To be here tonight—in the pits with a Super Stock—was to run with the big dogs.

Harlan eased the Blu hauler past the green Shaker State tractor-trailer of Rizer Racing family fame; on the other side of pit row was last year's points winner, Lonny Marzones, and beside him the black No. 12x of Jack Roverstein. The big rigs were lined up in even rows like checkers on a board. Their generators hummed like a choir stuck on one crazy note. Smoky had to park his motor home on the far side, though it was still within sight of the track. He kept his satellite dish folded down. Just after Team Blu found its slot, parked, and opened the big rear door, Cal Hopkins walked up.

"Whoa!" Trace murmured under his breath. Cal Hopkins was as famous as dirt track drivers got; he was the one who had spotted Trace at Headwaters Speedway, and also the one who had run last summer's Super Stock tryouts for Team Blu.

"Hey there, Trace," he said. Trim, wide-shouldered, and with silvery cropped hair, Hopkins looked like an old-school fighter pilot.

"Hi, Mr. Hopkins," Trace said.

Cal smiled. "Call me Cal. We're both racers now."

"Thanks," Trace said as they shook hands—though he still couldn't bring himself to call him Cal.

"Heard you been tearing it up out there," Cal said.

"Sort of," Trace said.

"Not sort of—for sure," Harlan said as he came forward to shake hands.

Jimmy hung back by the car; he was not good around famous people.

"I thought you'd do well," Cal said as he looked over the Blu Super Stock.

As they talked, Lonny Marzones walked by. "Cal!" he called, and the two men came together for a quick handshake and a man-hug. Marzones, also in his racing suit, was a stocky, round-faced guy with an easy smile.

"You know this kid?" Cal asked Lonny.

"Can't say as I do," Marzones said as he turned to Trace.

"Trace Bonham," Cal said. "He's an up-and-comer, a kid to keep your eyes on."

Trace and Marzones shook hands. "Nice rig for a Super Stock," Marzones said as he looked at the Blu hauler.

"Thanks," Trace said. Standing with Cal Hopkins and Lonny Marzones left him a quart low on words.

"Looks like you nailed a major sponsor. You guys should move up to sprints," Marzones said to Trace with a wink.

"We might be doin' that soon," Harlan said from inside the trailer. Jimmy, pretending to be busy, peeked over the side of the Super Stock.

"If there's time tonight, you should take a couple of laps in my backup car," Marzones said.

"Are you serious?" Trace blurted.

"Where else you going to learn?" Marzones said. "I'll mention it to my crew chief and the pit honcho. There's usually a break in the action at some point. A speedway should always have a car on the track, even if it's going around ten miles an hour."

"Ten?" Trace said.

Marzones gave Trace a friendly slap on the shoulder. "That's the spirit, son. If it's doable, I'll send somebody down later to get you," he said.

Cal and Marzones walked on, talking about the old days. When the two drivers were out of sight, Jimmy popped up from behind the blue Super Stock.

"Did you hear that?" he said.

"Yeah," Harlan said gruffly, as if nothing big had happened. "It's just racing."

Team Blu readied the Super Stock for time trials. No one from the Marzones team came by (Trace kept glancing down pit row), and eventually it was time to take the track.

After rolling up over the berm and down onto the black, tacky dirt of Rivers Speedway, Trace scrubbed the tires left and right—but there was little time to get relaxed: after one lap, the on-track flagman circled his finger, and Trace powered up for his time trial.

Maybe it was his Super Stock tryout here last summer, maybe it was the Blu car itself, maybe it was the lift from being among the top-dog racers—or maybe it was his time with Sara Thursday night. Whatever it was, the cockpit felt like an easy chair. Trace was loose and relaxed. There was no clear line between his body, the racing seat, the clutch, the accelerator, the gauges, and the tires. He pitched it hard through the corners, then ripped down the straightaways as if he owned the dirt. His laps were 16.45 and 16.39.

"All right," he shouted, punching the tin roof with a gloved fist. He came hot—too hot—into the pits. A steward gave him a universal palms-down wave, and Trace braked to a throaty idle down pit row. Back at the trailer, Harlan pretended to yawn as Trace rolled up to a stop.

Jimmy, slumped over, pretended to be dozing in his lawn chair.

"Real funny!" Trace said.

Harlan lunged forward to catch Trace's helmet, and Jimmy doubled up in a fit of laughter.

"Way to go out there," Harlan said, giving Trace a fist bump. "All you, kid!"

The comment brought Trace back to ground level. He looked across to Smoky's Gulf Stream. The little satellite dish was still down. "Yes," Trace said. "All me."

The time trials dragged on through the four classes: Super Stocks, Midwest Modifieds, Late Models, and finally sprints. But Rivers Speedway ran a tight ship, with one car accelerating onto the track as the previous one left. Trace and the Blu crew gathered at the fence to watch the sprint cars. The heavy concussions from their exhaust headers echoed inside Trace's ears even though he wore foam plugs. Watching the sprints at ground level made clear how powerful—and twitchy—they were. Too much throttle too quickly and it was instant spinout. But sprint cars were built to take the corners; drivers threw the cars into controlled, tire-spinning power drift, and torque and g-forces lifted the skinnier inside front tires until they only skimmed the dirt. On some cars, the left front tires dangled off the ground through the entire turn; on others, the smaller front tires dipped and tapped the dirt like eagles scooping fish from the surface of a lake.

"See that?" Harlan shouted, his voice almost noiseless in the roar. He was pointing at Lonny Marzones's car. "He keeps all four tires on the dirt."

Trace nodded.

Jimmy shouted, "It may look cool to show daylight under that tire, but you've got more control with all four on the ground."

Trace nodded. It made sense.

Suddenly someone tapped Trace hard on the shoulder. An ATV had come up close behind. "You Trace?" asked the driver, a guy about Trace's age; he remained on the ATV.

"Yes."

"Let's go. We've been looking all over for you," the driver said. He wore Lonny Marzones's cap and crew shirt.

"Yahoo!" Jimmy shouted.

Trace jumped onto the back of the ATV, and held on as they sped off to the Marzones hauler.

The Marzones crew chief was waiting, hands on his

hips, like an unhappy father. "I hate when Lonny does this," he said as Trace arrived.

Trace glanced uncertainly at the crew chief.

"That's Bob," the ATV driver murmured over his shoulder to Trace. "Don't take him too seriously."

Bob gestured for Trace to get off and come forward. "That's why it's called a backup car—so it's there if we need it," he said. "But you can have a couple of laps during intermission, before they start the heats."

"Great!" Trace said, trying not to sound too eager.

"He looks about the same general size as Lonny," the crew chief said to the others on the Marzones team. "Let's get him strapped in. Use some pads if his ass is too skinny."

If Trace's Super Stock cockpit was a tight fit, the sprint car's interior was tighter still—like being buckled into a straitjacket. He did end up sitting on some flex-foam pads that wrapped around his hips. "Use this helmet—it goes with our safety system," Bob said.

Trace pulled on a fresh Team Marzones helmet, then leaned forward to be fitted for a head and neck support (HANS) device; it was a sturdy fiberglass tongue that ran flat against his spine, upward to a stiff collar around his neck, which itself was hooked to several rings on Trace's loaner helmet, with its built-in receiver. "This system is designed to cut down your newtons," Bob said.

"My newtons?" Trace said.

"Not talking Fig Newtons here," Bob replied as a younger crew member stiffened Trace's range of head and neck movement. "Newton the scientist. G-forces are what kill you when you wreck—which you damn well better not."

"Don't worry," Trace said. He could look only a few degrees left or right; his arms had only inches of lateral movement.

"Worrying is what Lonny pays me for," the chief said gruffly as he watched his men work.

"He's good to go!" a crew guy said to Bob, who stepped forward and tugged at all the belts just to make sure.

Bob himself hooked up Trace's window net. "Okay, let's get this over with," he said to his crew.

The sprint car was push-start, and Trace concentrated on the starting sequence: transmission in gear (little lever on the right); fuel switch to On position.

"Ready?" Bob called.

Trace took a breath and gave a two-fingered wave forward.

A push truck bumped behind him and pressed Trace forward, down pit row. The sprint car's brake was a downpress pedal, not a forward leg-throw as in most cars—not that he planned on using much brake. As he approached the track entrance, Trace flipped the ignition switch to On—and the engine coughed alive.

Alone on the track, Trace idled along—no throttle applied—at somewhere close to thirty miles per hour. The 700-plus horsepower engine was less a motor than a force of nature—the rumbling inside an active volcano or the deep-lung cough of a far-off thunderstorm. The slightest tap to the gas pedal broke loose the rear tires: he had instant, unlimited power.

On his first lap he concentrated on keeping a consistent, steady pace through the turns and down the straights. He had watched enough sprint car action to know that slowing for corners was the sure sign of an amateur. He quickly completed two laps, but the on-track flagman did not wave him to the pits. The Marzones crew members and chief stood near the pit exit; on Trace's third lap, Bob circled a finger for him to bring up the speed— but slowly. Goose bumps washed over Trace's arms.

Gradually he built up speed to a half throttle. Fighting the impulse to slow for the turns, he pitched faster into them—and trusted the car. The gathering g-forces signaled "spinout!" but the squat, fat-tired car—pressed downward by the rooftop airfoil—twisted the high-banked clay turns like a waterslide car flung sideways through its curved chute. Trace plunged out of the corners and down the straightaway—with the next turn in his face within seconds.

He powered through the turns, fighting the feeling that the big tires were going to shred or roll over off their rims. Again he flashed by the Marzones crew, none of whom did anything but watch. He brought his speed up still more. By the fifth lap, he was running close to three-quarters throttle, and breaking off sharp, tight, controlled drifts through both ends of the track. He found a rhythm—an actual count inside his head—which helped him hit the corners just right and kept him from getting squirrelly out the back side.

The flagman threw the checkered, and the crew chief waved Trace in. He backed off immediately. Slowing, he took the engine out of gear before the pit exit, then coasted off the track with enough momentum to get partway down pit row. There he remembered to turn off the fuel switch. When the big engine starved and died, he switched the ignition to Off.

A local push truck rocked him from behind and rolled Trace the rest of the way to the Marzones hauler.

"Nothing to it, right?" Bob asked. His men unhooked the window net and began to unbuckle Trace.

"I wouldn't say that!" Trace answered, rolling his neck to loosen the muscles.

For the first time, Bob showed a hint of smile. "It was a trick question, kid."

Trace removed his helmet, which Bob stepped forward to take, and then Trace pulled himself backward from the cockpit. Lonny Marzones walked over, warm and sweaty-looking in his racing suit. "You must have a sprint car hidden away somewhere, right, son?"

"I wish," Trace said. He wanted to give Marzones a huge hug, but settled for a long, pumping handshake. "Thanks."

"You looked comfortable out there," Marzones said.

Trace let out two lungfuls of air. "I think I held my breath the whole time!"

The Marzones crew laughed—the good kind of laugh.

"We wouldn't have known by watching," Marzones said, "and that's the main thing. It's what we do—driving as in life—we try to make it look easy."

By then Harlan and Jimmy had arrived.

"What do you think, chief?" Marzones said to Harlan.

"About what? I was over getting a hot dog," Harlan said.

"Yeah, right," Trace said.

Marzones turned to his own crew chief. "How about you, Bobby?"

Bob quickly put his hard-boiled face back on. "He didn't wreck."

"Pay no attention to them," Marzones said to Trace with a smile. "I think you could move up tomorrow."

When Marzones was gone, Trace went to his cabin and called Mel. He had to tell somebody about his sprint car laps. She picked up on the first ring, and they talked for twenty minutes—until Harlan pounded on the door.

"Gotta go," Trace said.

"I wish I was there with you tonight," she said.

"Really?" Trace said stupidly.

"Really," she said. "Now go drive fast."

Trace's dream night continued in the heats. Starting second in the second heat, he maintained his placement—missing a checkered flag by a nose. His car was quick out of the corners but a half note slow down the straights. Still, a second place would put him well up to start the feature.

Smoky took the Blu Super Stock inside the hauler, so with time to kill, Trace wandered down pit row. He headed away from the big sprint car haulers—he was, after all, only a Super Stock driver—and gravitated toward the grassroots end of the pits. Pits had their pecking order. On the far side were the homemade flatbed trailers, the retrofitted furniture trucks, the worn-out but repainted tractor-trailer rigs. There was music and the smell of home-cooked food—burgers and barbecue—on grill kettles. Trailer doors were open wide, wives and husbands worked on their cars in front of God and everybody. Young motor heads hung close by the family race cars waiting for a chance to help. Family teams were laughing, arguing, working together. Trace found himself walking slower in order to listen, to take it all in.

"Hey, you look hungry," a large woman said. Behind a cloud of greasy smoke she was turning chicken wings on a propane grill. To the side was a beat-up gray Super Stock. The scene was like the old days, back at Headwaters Speedway when he drove his old Street Stock. When his dad was with him in the pits.

"No thanks. I've got to drive," Trace said.

She squinted and waved smoke away from her face. "Come by later, then. There might be leftovers," she said.

"Maybe I will," Trace said.

She looked more closely at him as the air cleared. "Hey, ain't you that Blu driver?"

"Yep," Trace said.

"The guy on the billboards."

"That's me."

She looked sideways to her team's flatbed trailer, where three guys pounded on a tire. They looked like a father and two grown sons—her family—but she didn't call to them; they were too busy telling one another how to get the tire off the rim. "So what brings you down to this end of the pits—the cheap seats?" she asked Trace with a throaty laugh. She kept turning chicken wings.

"I don't know," he said.

Something in his voice made her cock her head to look twice at him; she put down her tongs and stepped away from the grill and the smoke. Like that of the Carhartt lady, her face had seen some road, some weather. "Must be the down-home cooking," she said, wiping her hands on her apron.

"Must be," Trace said.

"Seriously, come by later. All you'd have to do is sit in a lawn chair and eat. My family is entertainment enough."

In the feature race, Trace started in the fourth row, inside. After the sprint car, his Super Stock felt wide and slow—like a school bus. But Jason Nelson, two rows back, was a good wake-up call; by lap 2, orange tin loomed in the dust and thunder just off Trace's right side. Nelson rocked him hard coming out of turn 4. Trace lost his line, and saw Nelson push past him on the high side. With full gas pedal, Trace spun and wallowed across the soft shoulder of the infield, kicking up chalk dust and barely missing a big bumper tire. When he fought his way back into traffic, he was running in the middle of the pack.

A restart on lap 10 closed up the field. As he bumped and tapped within the tight parade of cars leaning toward green, Trace heard himself say, "Come on, Smoky!"

His engine started to wake up on lap 12. It was nothing he could point to—not rpm or responsiveness in the throttle—but more like an increase in personality. The field had spread out, and Trace began to reel in cars one by one. He found bite on the high side, and better bite down low. Nelson was running third, but Trace set his sights not on him or the two cars ahead; rather, he began to race against the track. As long as he had room to move, he stayed on his best line and concentrated on nailing his lift spots; then it was hammer down, and out the far side of the turn. Focusing on the track rather than individual cars, Trace felt his lap times tightening—but running down the leaders was a gradual process. *If on a circular track Train A is averaging 80 miles per hour, and Train B, only three car lengths behind it, is averaging 82 mph, how long does it take Train B to catch Train A?*

Until lap 17.

Trace finally got tight behind Nelson—and began tapping his rear bumper pipe to get him loose. Nelson stayed on task and kept his line—making sure to swing his butt wide in the corners in order to take up two lanes. Trace finally got his nose inside Nelson's rear quarter panel, and held it there until he could make the pass down low.

After that, he had two laps to catch the leader. His engine kicked up another notch—he felt the surge this time. It was a strong enough punch that Trace threw a millisecond's glance sideways as he passed the pits. Smoky's motor home sat with satellite dish fully erect. Its cup pointed directly at Trace.

The fix was in.

With new power, Trace swung wide and streamed by the leader on the outside. He actually backed off the gas for the final lap, but still streamed under the checkered flag by two car lengths.

After his weigh-in, and the photo op, he headed to tech lane. There a small cluster of drivers—including old man Nelson—waited. Jason's father was out of control. He swore, kicked dirt, and jabbed his finger toward the Blu Super Stock.

The chief pit steward nodded and nodded, then gestured for Nelson to go away—back to his trailer. Jason Nelson hung to the side, watching.

"Great going, kid!" Harlan shouted over the engine noise.

Trace didn't reply.

"You ran them off the track tonight!"

Trace set his jaw. "Don't thank me," he muttered as he got ready for the usual tech circus.

"Huh?" Harlan said. "You drove the hell out of that car tonight."

"Yeah, well . . ." Trace began, but the pit steward walked up.

"I know, I know," Harlan said to him. "Take it to the tech shed."

"If you already know, what does that tell me?" the steward replied.

"It tells me, 'Hurry up and get done so we can pick up our check,' " Harlan replied.

Trace sat inside the car, as usual, as the tech guys swarmed over it. Being teched was like being in a traffic stop: take orders from the authorities, and say as little as possible. But after twenty minutes, the tech guys picked up their tools and walked away.

"Thank you," the tech chief said. "You're good to go."

"No—thank you!" Harlan said sarcastically.

When the Blu Super Stock returned to the hauler, Trace turned to look at Smoky's trailer. The satellite dish was down, folded up and put away.

"I need to talk to Smoky—and you, too!" Trace said. He was still cranked with postrace adrenaline—a swirl of emotions.

"Later," Harlan said. "You've got company."

Cal Hopkins and Lonny Marzones walked up to congratulate Trace. He did his best to put on a happy face. After that, a few fans lingered for autographs on 18x T-shirts, but the Modifieds were roaring, and Trace was soon finished.

"You wanted to talk to me?" Harlan asked.

Trace paused. Let out a breath. He was coming down from his checkered flag high—to a checkered flag low.

"Later," he said. "But for sure later."

"Okeydokey," Harlan said with a shrug.

Trace headed to his cabin, where he used the toilet, then sat on his bunk. He took some more deep breaths, and ate an apple. When he came downstairs, the Blu Super Stock was strapped down in travel position, and the big rear door was closed. There were men's voices outside, but no one was inside.

He stepped over to the car. He stared intently at the nearest hood pin. Just then voices from outside—Harlan's and Smoky's—grew louder, and the side door clattered. Smoky stepped in.

"Nice driving," he croaked to Trace.

"Thanks," Trace said. He turned to face him. "But I couldn't have done it without you."

There was a moment of dead airspace.

"None of us could do any of this without each other," Harlan said. "That's what a team is."

"Shucks, Pops, you're making me all weepy," Jimmy said from behind.

"Dry up," Harlan said.

With the hauler locked tight, and Smoky wearing his floppy hat and sunglasses, they all walked over to watch the Late Models—with a stop beforehand at the concession shack. Trace pretended that this was just another night at the speedway, but he glanced over his shoulder, back toward the Blu hauler. He touched his pocket to make sure he had his keys to the side door.

"I'll have the chicken with dirt," Harlan said to the plump girl.

"Got the chicken, dirt's free," she said. She was red-faced and steaming from the heat of the fryers, but still smiling.

"Nothing for you?" Harlan asked Trace.

"Stomach's a little iffy. I'll eat later," Trace said.

"Too much fun driving that sprint car," Smoky said.

When Harlan, Jimmy, and Smoky had their cardboard trays of food, they all made their way to the pit bleachers.

"Mmmmmmmm-mmmh!" Harlan said, sniffing the air. "The only smell better than speedway chicken is V-8 methanol."

"You're sure happy tonight," Smoky said to Harlan with his gravelly voice.

"Another feature win. Cal Hopkins and Lonny Marzones in our corner, life is good—eh, boys?" Harlan asked.

"Yahoom," Jimmy said, his mouth full.

"Sure," Trace said. "Life is great." He could feel Smoky's gaze.

"Big checkered flag, sprint car seat time—did you call your girlfriend yet?" Harlan asked.

"Which one?" Jimmy asked.

They all laughed—except Trace.

"His real girlfriend," Harlan said. "That tall, skinny blonde from Headwaters, the one who doesn't like us."

"Mel," Trace said.

"She's not that skinny," Jimmy said with appreciation.

"Yes, I called her," Trace said.

"I would, too," Harlan said.

During a restart in the Late Model feature, Trace gestured to the crew that he was heading over to the concession area. Harlan nodded and turned back to the action on the track. When the green flag dropped, and the cars strung out, the Blu crew's faces pitched left, right, left like those of spectators at a tennis match. Trace started toward the concessions; then, after one more glance behind, he headed back to the Blu hauler.

With his key he let himself inside. The Blu Super Stock hood was still warm. He carefully unpinned it. Setting it aside, he removed the circular air cleaner, then leaned close to the carburetor. A Holley two-barrel. Standard issue—at least from outward appearances. He looked at it from all sides, and even took some cell phone photos of it from all directions—especially down the throat. Why he took pictures, he wasn't sure: if experienced track tech guys couldn't see an issue, how was he supposed to?

He buttoned the hood, making sure to position the four bonnet pins exactly as they had been. Then he straightened up and looked around the trailer at the various tool drawers labeled REAR END and STEERING and BRAKES and more—including two padlocked drawers marked SMOKY. He squinted to look closer, then bent down. A flat metal washer about the size of a dime was stuck on the outside of the first drawer. With a fingernail, Trace pried it loose—but the washer didn't fall to the floor. It swapped sides and went *clack!* back against the steel-sided drawer. Trace tried it again. The magnetic pull of the drawer front was strong enough to suck the washer from the palm of his hand: *schwack!*

Just then a key slid into the lock; Trace scrambled away from the drawer. He managed to be rummaging in the BATTERIES drawer when Smoky stepped inside.

"Find what you're looking for?" he asked in his sandpaper voice.

"I need some batteries—triple A—for my TV remote."

Smoky looked around the trailer, as if making sure everything was in place. Then he said, "I thought you were hungry."

"Can't take the grease," Trace said. "Thought I'd grab some snacks from my fridge."

"So you're going to watch TV while the races are on?" Smoky asked.

"I just wanted to check the NASCAR results."

Smoky paused. "There's double A batteries in there but not triple A."

"No big deal," Trace said, turning away. "I'll find some later."

As he headed to the cabin door, Smoky watched him all the way. "You forgot your snacks," he said.

In the sprint car feature, several local sprint cars joined the World of Outlaws on the track, but they didn't have the engines to compete. Still, the local fans cheered for the "farmers," as Harlan called the independent cars, one of which—the Moffett Farms sprint—hung tough in the middle of the pack. But the World of Outlaws cars gradually took over the top ten or so places. Lonny Marzones and Larry Rizer had a hard bump in the far turn, spinning Marzones through white chalk dust and into the infield. As yellow lights flashed and the sprints rolled along under the caution flag, Marzones's car sat dead. A push truck, lights flashing, quickly tucked in behind—but Marzones waved him off. The driver and two on-track officials crouched to look underneath Marzones's car—then one of them waved for a tow truck. One sped over, then backed up, cable dangling, and hoisted Marzones's front end off the ground.

"Damn," Trace said. "He was running third."

On the hook, Marzones got a free, slow ride back to the pits. Trace and Team Blu left the pit bleachers, and were waiting with the Marzones crew when Lonny arrived. His right front tire dangled like a bird's broken wing. Behind, the race thundered up without him.

"All right, boys, you know the drill," Bob said to the crew. He seemed almost cheerful.

"Tough luck," Marzones called, tossing out his helmet. "Larry and I got our signals crossed in turn 2."

"Looked that way," Bob said.

"Oh well, that's racing," Marzones said, his voice muffled as he pulled himself out. Then he stood and hitched himself upward in a little shimmy that most drivers did (if they were male) when they got out of the car. He spotted Trace to one side.

"What do you think, Trace?" he said.

"I liked it," Trace answered. "Up until you got hammered."

Marzones shrugged. "You got to like it all, son," he said, "because a bad day at the track is better than a good day in real life—ain't that right, boys?"

His crew laughed as they worked on the car, and Marzones disappeared into his trailer.

Trace met his father again after the races. He had driven over to the speedway alone—no Linda this time.

"You want to get something to eat?" Trace asked.

"Sure!" his father said. He seemed surprised.

They headed down to Whitey's Café, near the Red River and the flood dikes.

"Did you happen to notice that Marzones car all alone out there during intermission?" Trace asked.

"Yes. He must have been tuning and testing."

"That was me in the car," Trace said.

His father's brown eyes widened. "Are you kidding?"

Trace couldn't hold back a grin. He told his dad the whole story.

"Damn! That is *something*!" his father said. "You looked great out there!"

"It went all right," Trace said.

"Jeez, Son, you'll be running with the big dogs before we know it!" His father drummed his fingers sharply on the table.

Trace was silent. Then he glanced around the café, and back to his father. "Can I ask you something?"

"Sure, Son—anything."

"Have you ever cheated?"

His father drew back slightly; his gaze flickered sideways, then back to Trace. "You mean, like, cheated on your mother?"

"No—not that," Trace said quickly. "I mean in business."

His father took a moment to answer. "I once bought an eighty real cheap from this old farmer because he didn't get along with his family, and he didn't like real estate agents. Called them 'bloodsuckers,' and threatened to shoot the next agent who showed up. He sold it to me just to spite everybody else."

"But it's not like you lied to the old guy," Trace said.

"No. I was in the right place at the right time—like you with this racing thing, Son."

Trace toyed with a little creamer cup.

"Why? Is something wrong?" his father asked.

Trace shrugged. "Sort of," he began. "All I'm allowed to do is drive. They never let me even look at the engine."

"Lonny Marzones doesn't work on his engines," his father said.

"I'm not Lonny Marzones," Trace said.

"True," his father said. "But you have a professional team behind you."

"Yeah," Trace said, lowering his voice. "But some nights we have way too much engine."

His father was silent.

"It's like we're running a four-barrel carb. Or something . . ." Trace trailed off.

"Have you had any trouble in the tech inspections?" his father asked.

"No."

"Well, there you have it," his father said, leaning back. "You're probably still not used to a genuine, pro-built motor."

Trace took a sip of his water.

"And anyway," his father continued, "most people would say it's the driver who wins races—not the car."

The waitress came with their steaks. Trace's dad flashed her his big smile, but she was looking shyly at Trace. "More water?"

"Sure," Trace said.

She returned with a pitcher. As she poured, she blurted, "You look just like that race-car guy on the Blu commercials."

"He is that guy," Trace's father said.

"Oh my gosh!" the waitress said with a tiny shriek.

"Please," Trace said to his father.

"Well, you are him," his father said to Trace. It was like his father hadn't heard any good news for a long time.

The waitress blushed deeply—and sloshed water from her pitcher. "Oh shoot!" she said.

"Hey, it's all right," Trace said, grabbing a napkin.

"Don't worry about it—it's only water," his father said.

As the waitress went away, Trace's father's eyes dropped briefly to her backside. "What a sweetheart," he said.

Trace let it ride—the waitress and the motor thing. The moment was past.

10

Sunday night brought Team Blu into Minnesota, and Buffalo River Race Park. Just east of Moorhead on Highway 10, it was a sticky black-gumbo, quarter-mile oval with a freshly remodeled white metal grandstand. A driver favorite—Trace had raced here before—Buffalo River was also where he had met April, who worked in the concession stand. They had seen each other a couple of times, though not recently. He had stopped returning her calls.

"Jimmy, do me a favor," Trace said. Team Blu was parked in the pits, and the concession stand was now open.

"Sure."

Trace leaned in and murmured his request.

"You mean that chick April, from the last time we were here?" Jimmy said.

"Yes," Trace said, glancing around. "See if she's working here tonight."

"And if she is, what do I say?"

"Nothing," Trace said. "The main thing is, I don't want to see her."

"Jeez! Why not?" Jimmy asked quickly.

"Just . . . because," Trace said. "So be cool. Order some food, whatever. It's not like she's going to recognize you."

"She might," Jimmy said, straightening his cap and slicking back his hair as he walked off.

"What's that all about?" Harlan asked from behind the Super Stock.

"Nothing," Trace replied.

Race teams continued to roll in, including Jason Nelson—and then Sara Bishop and her father with their Super Stock. Jason flashed a longhorn salute as he passed by, but Sara's father, with their car on the trailer, stopped to talk. He was friendly, as always; Sara had little to say. After an awkward silence, she looked toward the big Blu hauler. "Anybody from Headwaters coming over to see you race tonight?"

"I don't think so," Trace said.

"Well, see you on the track, I guess," she said finally.

"Okay. Good luck," Trace said.

She motioned for her father to drive on.

"Wasn't that the girl in the Chevelle from the other night?" Harlan asked.

"Yes," Trace said.

"She didn't seem all that happy," Harlan said.

A couple of Super Stock teams from Headwaters rattled past, including Gerry Harkness and his family. There had been bad blood at the end of last season; Gerry drove a local Super Stock at Headwaters, and had been the first to protest Trace's Team Blu motor. But this afternoon, Gerry blustered over, big smile on his face, his wife and kid in tow.

"Hey, Mr. Big Shot," Gerry said. He had larger hands and arms than Harlan, but fewer teeth. "Just can't get away from you!"

"Hi, Gerry," Trace said, and greeted his family as well.

"Billboards, those TV ads—and now we gotta run into you here," Gerry said, and sighed.

"Sorry about that," Trace said.

"Why ain't you on *American Idol*, that's what I want to know."

" 'Cause he can't sing," Harlan said from the side.

"I'll bet he can," Gerry said. He was one of those guys whose humor was always on the edge—friendly jabs that could tip either way. "Let's hear something."

"No chance," Trace said.

At that moment Jimmy appeared. "No," he mouthed to Trace.

Trace nodded.

"No what?" Harlan asked. The Harkness family looked on.

Trace turned to the Harknesses. "How's the speedway makeover going back home?"

Gerry winced. "Slow. I hope Mel's not in over her head. Johnny gave her the green light, and it's too late to turn back now."

"It's going to be a great track once it's done," Gerry's wife, Cindy, said.

"If it ever gets done," Gerry said.

"Ain't you going to ask about his cheater motor?" the Harkness kid said to his dad.

There was silence but for the pit sounds.

"That was last season," Gerry said. "We turned the page, right, Trace?"

"Good luck tonight, Gerry," Trace said.

As the Harkness family moved on, Jimmy whispered, "I asked around about April, but she's not working tonight," he said.

"Thanks." Trace did not know whether to be relieved or disappointed. He checked his watch, then sat in Jimmy's lawn chair and caught some sun while the crew worked—the crew except Smoky, who remained in his motor home. The sounds of NASCAR radio came from inside. When Harlan went inside the hauler, Trace suddenly got up and followed him.

"What would we need magnets for?" Trace asked Harlan. He kept his voice down.

"Magnets?" Harlan asked. He turned to stare.

"I noticed something strange," Trace said, pointing to the padlocked drawers. He fished a metal washer out of a can and knelt beside the steel compartments. "Watch this." He tossed the washer—which went *tack!* against the drawer front, and hung there.

Harlan stared. Then he stepped over, bent down, and peeled off the washer. "Those are Smoky's drawers," he said.

"I know that, but—"

"But nothing," Harlan said. "Just leave well enough alone."

"There's something weird going on with my motor," Trace said. He blocked Harlan's path back to daylight.

"Weird?" Harlan asked.

"Yeah. That's what I wanted to talk about last night."

"What do you mean, 'weird'? Smoky's motors run great."

"Yeah, well, sometimes they run too great. It's like Smoky gives me power when he wants to, or when I really need it—like last night in the last few laps."

Harlan stared. "Have you been watching those late-night religious channels?"

"Huh?" Trace asked.

"Smoky ain't God," Harlan continued. "He can't just fill your motor with the Holy Spirit whenever he wants to."

Trace glanced at the Blu Super Stock, then at the old Gulf Stream. "Maybe, maybe not."

Harlan gave Trace a long look. "You just drive, remember?" he said. "And don't be snooping around Smoky's stuff."

Just then a track guy came along on an ATV. "Drivers' meeting! Drivers' meeting!" he called.

"You got that? Is that clear?" Harlan asked.

"All right, all right!" Trace muttered, and walked away.

At the prerace gathering of drivers, the chief pit steward, wearing a headset and a green safety vest, stood atop an ATV. He held a bullhorn and waited impatiently for the drivers. It was standard procedure at every speedway for a track official to read off the general rules, and to orient drivers new to the speedway. It was also standard procedure for drivers to be in no hurry to gather; they joshed with one another, played little mind games, talked cars, and fished for information as they slowly migrated toward the bullhorn.

Jason Nelson and his father were already there. The older Nelson stood with a group of drivers, all of whom swiveled their heads to look at Trace. He ignored them and paused center-back, where he folded his arms and waited for the usual sermon.

"Let's go, let's go!" the official called to the drivers still on their way. "We do have to race tonight." He was crabby, like all chief pit stewards, but getting race drivers to follow instructions was like rounding up cats and dogs.

"New drivers: you go on the track in turn 2, you go off on turn 1," he began, and continued with restart and then return-to-the pit rules. "On a yellow flag, a driver with a flat or minor mechanical trouble may return to the pits while the other cars complete two slow laps under caution. If you can make it back, fine, but we drop the green flag after two laps—any questions?"

There were none. Everything was standard procedure. As the race director went on, Trace gradually felt something strange. He looked behind, then to his right, then to his left. In the crowd of over fifty drivers, no one stood within ten feet of him. The chief pit steward began to stare at Trace—or rather, try not to stare. He swung his bullhorn right, then left, but purposefully didn't aim it toward Trace—who stood like an outcast animal at the edge of the herd.

Jason Nelson broke away from his father, and ambled across the open space toward Trace. He stopped nearby, folded his arms across his chest as if bored like everyone else, and continued to listen. The circle of faces gradually turned back to the race director.

"Hey," Trace said. It was the least he could do.

"Hell, ah know it ain't you," Jason said under his breath.

Trace looked briefly sideways, but didn't answer.

"It's your engine guy," Jason continued, all the while watching the race director.

Trace concentrated on saying nothing.

"It's like he holds you back in the heats, then juices your motor for the feature," Jason said. "Everybody knows."

"Juices it?" Trace said.

Other drivers turned to stare.

"Yeah. Or whatever it is he does," Jason said, not caring who heard.

"Something for sure," his father said from nearby. "Ain't no Super Stock should run like yours does."

"We're having a meeting here!" the race director said, his bullhorn louder.

"Money talks," Harlan called to Jason and his father. "Like I always say, if you think we're cheating, put up two hundred dollars and protest our engine."

Heads turned as Harlan shouldered his way through the crowd.

"We may be dumb, but we're not stupid," Jason's father said.

"Too bad there's not an engine-claiming rule in Super Stock class," another driver said. "Then we'd see if you could win with my motor."

"If you don't mind—" the race director boomed.

But the drivers were all focused on Trace. "That's probably why Team Blu runs Super Stocks," someone said. "They couldn't win with somebody else's motor."

"Or maybe you boys just don't know how to build engines—let alone set up a car right!" Harlan growled as he stood next to Trace.

"I can handle this," Trace muttered.

"Go back to the trailer," Harlan replied.

Trace stepped away, angry and humiliated, but didn't leave.

"Hey, don't get your shorts in a wad!" a local driver said to Harlan. "We're just sayin' what everybody thinks."

"Do your talking on the track," Harlan replied.

"We're talkin' right here, you fat redneck!" another driver called.

"Okay, that's enough!" the race director boomed. "I'm calling the six-foot rule right now!"

Two pit stewards in green safety vests hustled toward the tightening group of drivers and crew members, which quickly broke apart at their approach. Jason Nelson disappeared like a gopher down a hole. The six-foot rule was designed to prevent just such in-your-face confrontations between drivers; it carried fines, point losses—even disqualification.

"We'll see your boy on the track!" a driver called over his shoulder to Harlan.

"You might see his rear end if you're lucky," Harlan shot back.

Back at the trailer, Harlan sat down in his lawn chair and lit a cigarette. He drew deeply, then turned to Trace. "Want one?"

"No," Trace said.

"That's the right answer," Harlan said. "These things will kill you."

Trace was silent.

"If they don't kill me, these farmers might," Harlan added, looking around the pits.

Trace followed his gaze. "So why do we run Super

Stocks?" he asked suddenly. "If we ran Modifieds, we'd have way more places, way more speedways to race. Maybe they're right about the claimer class."

Harlan barked out a short laugh, and spit to the side. "It's way simpler than that. The higher-ups, like Laura Williams? They thought Super Stocks would look cooler on billboards than other car types. Super Stocks are longer, bigger—more tin for advertising."

"More tin?" Trace asked. "That's the only reason?"

"Yep," Harlan said. "That engine no-claim rule just fell into our laps."

Trace was silent.

Harlan glanced at him. "In racing, when a rule falls your way, you make it work for you. Squeeze it, stretch it, find the gray area, find the space inside it where you can operate."

"Which is what Smoky does," Trace said.

"I don't know what Smoky does," Harlan said, and sucked again on his cigarette. "I only know that he gets you a lot of horsepower. I don't ask, and Smoky sure as hell don't tell."

Just as Trace opened his mouth, Harlan said, "And you don't need to know, either. You're winning. You got the world by the short hairs, kid. Leave things alone."

"Yeah. But all the other drivers want to wreck me."

"They wreck you, we got another car," Harlan said.

"That only pisses them off more."

"Which makes them worse drivers," Harlan said.

"Still—" Trace began.

"Still nothing," Harlan said, cutting him off. "Let me give it to you straight: do you want to be Mr. Nice Guy? Or do you want to win?"

Trace was silent. He picked up a pebble, then pitched it away.

"Lemme tell you another thing," Harlan said. "You're on the racing radar now. Lonny Marzones, other people— they've got their eyes on you. They think you might be the real deal."

"What about you?" Trace said.

"Once in a blue moon, I do, too," Harlan said gruffly.

Trace was silent.

"Stock car racing is like any other sport—there are scouts everywhere," Harlan continued. "If there's some farm kid out of Podunk, North Dakota, who can throw a baseball through a barn wall, some scout's watching him. If there's a skinny city kid in Chicago who can dunk the basketball in sixth grade, some scout's got him in his computer. Well, you're a young dirt track driver they're watching."

"Who's 'they'?"

"You don't need to know," Harlan said. "All you need to do is drive like you've been doing, and leave the rest to me and Smoky."

Trace headed to his cabin—where he wanted to break or kick something—but just then his phone beeped. It was a text from Jimmy: RED ALERT GIRL.

Trace stepped to his cabin window—and saw Mel walking down pit row. He froze. She was the last thing he'd expected tonight.

He looked around the cabin. The first thing that came to mind was to brush his teeth. He gave them a five-second brush, spit, rinsed, then hustled downstairs—slowing at the hauler side door so as not to seem surprised or eager.

She was smiling as she came toward the Blu hauler. Mel was always taller in real life than she was inside his head (she should have been a basketball or volleyball player). Her jeans were nicer and tighter than usual, but otherwise she wore her standard speedway outfit: World of Outlaws cap with blond ponytail poking out the back, sunglasses, and a Trace Bonham T-shirt.

"Surprise!" she called.

"Wow—that's for sure!" he said as he came forward to meet her. "I thought you had to work tonight."

"I changed my mind," she said. "Girls get to do that."

"I'm glad," Trace said. They paused a long step apart. "Nice T-shirt," he added.

"I know the guy," she said. "Sort of."

They both stepped forward at the same moment and had a major hug. He could not help burying his face briefly against her neck. She always smelled good; today it was like flowers—clover or lavender.

"Did your dad come?" Trace asked. Johnny Walters was a former sprint car driver, now in a wheelchair; together he and Mel ran Headwaters Speedway.

"No. Just me." Mel's face colored slightly.

"Great," Trace said. He glanced behind; Jimmy was working too quietly underneath the car, Harlan was conveniently out of sight inside the hauler, and Smoky's side window was cracked open a few inches. "Let's walk," Trace said.

As they headed toward the grandstand, Gerry Harkness called out, "Hey, Mel—when's our speedway going to be done?"

She waved. "Soon. Fourth of July at the very latest."

"We can't wait," Gerry's wife said.

"Fourth of July? Me neither," Trace murmured.

Mel ignored him. "Construction is pretty much on schedule," she said to the Harknesses. "The grandstands get knocked down next week. New aluminum bleachers are coming."

"You should have a workday," Gerry said. "Put out a call for all the drivers and their crews to help pick rocks or pound nails, whatever."

"I like the idea! I'll be in touch," Mel said.

As they walked on, Mel said softly, "I can't wait until the Fourth of July, either—which is why I drove over here tonight." She spoke quickly, as though she needed to say it now or it wouldn't get said.

Trace stumbled to a halt.

"I'm staying over," she said.

"Overnight?"

She nodded.

"Where?" Trace asked.

"Well, I have an aunt in Fargo, but my nieces and nephews are way wild," she said. "So I got a motel room."

"A motel?" Trace said.

"Yes. They're places where people pay to stay?" she teased.

Trace heard himself mouth-breathing. "Are you serious?" he said. His voice was suddenly croaky.

She laughed, but blushed deeply at the same time. "You clearly weren't listening. I just said, 'I can't wait until the Fourth of July, either.' "

"Wow," Trace said.

"Do you need to sit down?" Mel said. "You're not going to faint on me?"

"I might," Trace said. He put his arms around her.

She turned away from his kiss. "Ummm, this is not the motel," she said, but let him hold her.

"Maybe I'll ditch the races tonight," Trace said.

"Yeah, right!" she said. She broke away and pulled him along, her arm through his. At concessions, she ordered a major tray of food, including a taco in a bag and a large cola, after which they sat in the stands. They watched the Pure Stocks and the Bombers, but Trace couldn't concentrate on the track.

"What?" Mel said.

Trace turned to her. "I wonder if Harlan would let Jimmy drive tonight."

"Are you crazy? And anyway, your boss, Laura, wouldn't like it," Mel said.

"She wouldn't have to know."

"As if that witch wouldn't find out," Mel said; she was not a fan of Laura—her red lipstick, short skirts, and silky business blouses.

"You're probably right," Trace said.

"You just do your thing on the track like always," Mel said. "The faster you drive, the sooner your race will be over. Think of it that way."

In his heat race, Trace drove like a crazy man, spinning out once, pressing too hard, and finishing seventh of eight cars.

"What the hell?" Harlan asked as Trace hoisted himself up from the cockpit.

"Sorry, my fault," Trace said.

"No kidding," Harlan said.

"Got in a hurry," Trace said, wiping sweat from his face. Mel lingered across pit row; she had been watching from along the fence, and did not come over now. She was also not a fan of Harlan—he had insulted most everyone at Headwaters Speedway on Team Blu's one and only stop there.

"You can't win a race on the first lap—you know better than that," Harlan said.

"Don't know what I was thinking," Trace said, his gaze drifting to Mel's long legs and tight jeans.

"I do," Harlan said, following Trace's look. "We should have a damn rule: no girls in the pits before the races."

"What about after?" Trace said.

"After is fine," Harlan said, then realized that Trace was joking—but only slightly.

Trace glanced once more at Mel, then stepped closer to Harlan. Keeping his voice low, he explained the situation.

"Holy moly!" Harlan said, looking over at Mel.

"I told you not to look!" Trace said.

"Sorry," Harlan said, focusing back on Trace. He manufactured a pained look. "You know I like to hit the road right after the feature, but, all things considered . . ." His gaze sneaked sideways to Mel.

In the feature, thanks to a bad draw and his poor heat finish, Trace rolled toward the green flag in the ninth row, outside. There were only two cars behind him. Sara Bishop was in the middle of the pack, and Jason Nelson in the third row, inside. Impatiently, Trace drummed the throttle, breaking loose the rear tires again and again. He pressed close against the car ahead. As the lead car dropped the hammer and surged forward, Trace broke to the outside. He loved this Buffalo River black gumbo, and the Blu Super Stock, thanks to Jimmy's tire and setup magic, clawed past several cars. However, the higher Trace went the looser he got, so he backed off slightly. He probed down low for a crack, a sliver of daylight between cars—like trying to merge into heavy freeway traffic on a day when all the drivers were pissed off. A local white car rocked Trace—forcing him higher—but Trace pulled away, and the other car fell back. The other Super Stocks were equally happy to pinch off or bump Trace's car. His Blu Super Stock had an invisible bull's-eye stuck on it tonight.

After another hard thump, Trace muttered, "Okay, we can do that!" He hit back hard as he forced his way into the flow. His left front fender tin tore loose and began to flap—but didn't fly off. It chattered against his left front tire—sharp tin rubbing the sidewall rubber—and a half lap later sliced through the tire like a knife blade popping a balloon. The Super Stock shuddered and slewed. Trace cranked the car sideways—a calculated spinout—which brought out the caution flag. Without slowing, he high-tailed it to the pits, flat tire thundering inside the wheel well as the rubber plies tore apart.

Jimmy was waiting with a floor jack and a fresh tire mounted on a new wheel. Trace sat, engine revving, while Jimmy air-hammered the lug nuts partway loose, lurched the front end off the ground with the jack, then zipped off the nuts and clattered on the new wheel. As he worked, Harlan used a rivet gun on the loose fender tin. Jimmy's air hammer rattled like a crazy woodpecker.

"Go!" Jimmy shouted. Trace humped the Super Stock off the jack, and burned his tires back down pit row.

He powered onto the track in the nick of time: the green flag was down, and he dove into line just ahead of the lead car—which meant he was a full lap behind. "Let's do it!" he said to himself, and concentrated on racing against the track, not the other cars. There were still twelve laps to go in the twenty-five-lap feature. Trace drove hard and smart, taking advantage of another yellow flag to pick up several places.

On lap 16 a green Super Stock tangled with somebody, rode up over a front wheel, then flipped twice. It happened just ahead of Trace—he dove low to avoid wrecking himself. The green car landed upside down in front of the grandstand in an explosion of dust and flapping metal. Red lights flashed, and the cars stopped dead as EMTs raced to the upside-down pile of a Super Stock. The driver, a local guy, emerged unhurt but staggering, to a standing ovation. His car was wrecked. Totaled. As he put both hands on the flattened roof and lowered his head, Trace flashed on the late-night waitress back in Iowa: her comments on family life, racing, and money.

After a long delay (which helped him get his mind right), Trace powered up, and the remaining cars rumbled forward again under yellow. In the thunder following green, Trace soon clawed his way back to the middle of the pack—right beside Sara. He gave her plenty of room, however. This race was about finishing, not winning; if he caused a second yellow flag, he was done for the night. However, the engine found a sweet spot, Jimmy's tire setup was fist-in-glove rubber to dirt—so on lap 20 he went for it.

Sara pinched him hard, but Trace got by her down low. After that it was Gerry Harkness—who also rocked him—

and eventually Trace rode the orange bumper pipes of Jason Nelson. On the next lap, Trace got his nose between Nelson and a green Super Stock. The cars glued up three-wide through the turn—Trace caught a flash in his side vision of the crowd jumping to its feet—then powered down the straightaway. Trace felt his engine quicken—like some kind of overdrive—and he gradually pulled away by a car length, and then two. By the white-flag lap he had two more cars to pass, which he did with a sweet high-low dive. His engine thrummed at 8500 rpm, with still more left—but he didn't need it. He took the checkered by three car lengths.

In victory lane, the trophy girl (there was always a new one) hung on tight, smiling as the crowd booed. Trace held up a fist, a victory salute—which only brought louder boos.

"Don't worry, I like you," the trophy girl said.

"You might be the only one," Trace said as the cameras continued to flash.

"You got a girlfriend?" the trophy girl asked.

"Yes."

"A real one?"

"Very," Trace said. "She's waitin' for me in the pits."

After the photos, Trace headed to the tech lane. "Don't see many guys go last to first after a flat tire," a scruffy tech guy said—and motioned Trace toward the tech shed.

There Trace, Harlan, and Jimmy stood around while the tech guys did their thing. The pits were shadowy enough that even Smoky stood nearby. Mel lingered opposite Smoky, and as the teardown stretched on, Trace walked out to her.

"I see what you meant about your motor," she whispered. She glanced sideways at Smoky.

"Yeah," Trace said. Arms folded, he stared into the tech shed as the men worked with wrenches, trouble lights, and micrometers. "But they never find anything out of spec."

Mel was silent. Then she ventured, "Maybe it's not—"

"It has to be," Trace said. "Nobody has a Super Stock motor that runs like Smoky's."

They watched in silence.

"So what are you going to do?" Mel asked.

"I just drive," Trace said, a hard edge in his voice. "And I keep winning."

After a few more minutes the head tech guy stepped away from the car and turned toward Harlan. "Thanks—and have a nice day," he said.

Trace looked sideways toward Smoky, but he was gone.

The tech crew gathered up their tools, leaving a mess of Blu V-8 heads, pushrods, gaskets, valve covers, and an oil pan.

"You fine gentlemen have a great day, too!" Harlan said with exaggerated politeness.

"I gotta go," Trace said to Mel. "See you back at the hauler."

"Then you're done for the night?" Mel asked.

Trace blinked. He had almost forgotten that part—but certainly wasn't going to tell her. "Yes. Ten minutes and we're out of here."

With a push truck behind, Trace steered the dead Super Stock down pit row. Most of the other teams had buttoned up their cars and gone to the concession area for food or to the stands to watch the races. Trace coasted up to the Blu hauler, where a few people waited, and pulled himself out. Smoky was nowhere to be seen.

"Hey, Trace—can I get a driver's card?" a kid called.

"Trace, can you sign my T-shirt?" another boy asked.

Trace took care of business while Jimmy opened the big rear door and then hooked up the winch cable. The electric motor whirred as Harlan and Jimmy, working from the back of the trailer, maneuvered the Super Stock inside.

"Great driving," said a woman's deep voice. It was the chicken-wing lady he'd met the night before at the other end of the pits at Rivers Speedway.

"Thanks," Trace said cautiously.

She stepped up to Trace. "It's not for me to say what's in your engine, but after the reception you got, I didn't think you'd be walking through the pits—so I brought you some chicken wings."

Trace swallowed. "Thanks," he said, and took the foil package, which was still warm. He felt a weird burning in his eyes—like he could cry—but he fought it off.

"Shirley," she said.

"Thanks a lot, Shirley."

"Who was that?" Harlan said from the side. He straightened to watch the woman walk away.

"Just some lady."

" 'Just some lady'? And you took a package of chicken wings from her?"

"I talked to her last night," Trace explained, but then stopped.

"Hey, Trace, can I get a picture with you?" a skinny young girl in a racing cap asked. She was all teeth and elbows; her mother stood poised with a camera.

"Sure," Trace said. He handed the wings to Jimmy, and knelt down for the flash.

Mel had arrived, and watched from the side. When Trace was finally done, he turned her way and waved.

"No, I don't want a photo," Mel called.

"Very funny," Trace said.

"We're going to get some food," Harlan called to Trace. "Smoky—are you coming?"

"Okay," Smoky rasped from close behind his motor home window screen. He was always watching, listening.

"How about you, kid?" Harlan asked Trace.

"No."

Harlan and Jimmy turned to look at Mel, waiting a few yards away. Harlan made an exaggerated point of checking his watch. "Okay. We won't leave without you."

"Thanks, boss," Trace said sarcastically.

"Hey—are you going to eat these wings?" Jimmy said

to Trace, munching on one as he powered up the big rear door.

"Not now," Trace said.

Smoky emerged, carefully locked his motor home door, and then he and Jimmy and Harlan headed toward the concessions.

Now that they were finally alone, Trace turned to Mel, who came forward to the Blu hauler. "I need to change before we go," he said. "Want to come inside?"

"Good girls never go into a rock star's motor home or a race driver's cabin," Mel said. "But I guess I could—this once."

The side service door of the hauler was unlocked, and Mel followed Trace inside, and up the little stairs. Trace pushed open his door—then froze.

"Hey, Trace. The door was open." It was April, the girl from the concessions stand, lying on his bed in jeans and a very tight, very full, blue and white 18x T-shirt.

Mel stumbled against Trace, who tried—stupidly—to block her view. But it was too late. There was a long moment as Mel stared at April. April stared back.

"Oh dear—I guess I should have called ahead," April said.

"Yeah, me too!" Mel said—and spun around to leave.

"Wait," Trace said.

"Go to hell," Mel called over her shoulder. Her feet pounded down the stairs and out of the trailer. Its door slammed hard.

11

When Harlan returned, Trace was sitting in his lawn chair beside the trailer, smoking one of Harlan's cigarettes.

"What the—?" Harlan began.

"Let's go," Trace said. "Let's hit the road."

Harlan glanced sideways at Jimmy and Smoky. Smoky disappeared into the Gulf Stream. "Gimme that thing," Harlan said. He yanked the cigarette from Trace's hand.

Trace stared across the nearly empty pits to the headlights moving on Highway 10.

"Where's your girl?" Harlan asked.

"Gone," Trace said. "Probably for good." He slumped forward in the chair, and stared at the ground.

"What the hell happened?" Harlan asked.

Trace looked up at Jimmy. "You said April wasn't here."

"What?" Jimmy exclaimed. "No way! She ain't working here, and I never saw her anywhere."

"Well, she was here—in my cabin," Trace said.

"Damn!" Jimmy said with a pained look.

"But hey, that's not really Jimmy's fault, is it?" Harlan said.

"No," Trace said. "No, it's not." Across the empty pits, an eighteen-wheeler rumbled west on the highway.

Harlan pulled up a chair. He sat down. He drew deeply on Trace's cigarette. "I shouldn't have joked about fence bunnies the other day."

Trace had no words.

"I could talk to her if you like," Harlan said. "Tell her you're not that kind of guy."

"I am that kind of guy," Trace said.

"I wouldn't say that," Harlan said. "You're handling this whole thing—the billboards, the fans, the attention— way better than I would have. Way better than most guys I know. I'd be like a kid in a candy shop—I'd be knocking over chicks like bowling pins. You're not that way—and you're a damn good driver, too."

"I want to win—but on my own!" Trace blurted.

Harlan jerked his head at Jimmy, who disappeared into Smoky's motor home. When he was gone, Harlan took another long draw. "You could win on your own. You're a good enough driver," he said.

"So we *are* cheating," Trace said.

"I didn't say that," Harlan said. "You're the one who says that."

"You don't drive the car," Trace shot back. "You don't feel what I feel on the pedal. You don't see what I see on the tach."

Harlan was silent for a moment. "Okay, okay—fair enough." He lowered his voice to a near-whisper. "I know Smoky's up to something. Nobody knows Chevy motors like Smoky, but I swear on my momma's grave I don't know what he's doing."

"It has something to do with carburetion—" Trace began.

"And I don't want to know," Harlan interrupted.

"Maybe a combination of the fuel pump and the carb," Trace continued, "because it's definitely about fuel flow."

"Unless you can tell me exactly what he's doing, I don't want to hear about it!" Harlan said.

Trace fell silent.

Harlan let out a long exhale of cigarette smoke. They sat in silence for at least a minute. Then Harlan spoke. "Let me tell you something Darrell Waltrip once said about racing. It was pretty close to this: 'If you don't cheat, you're an idiot. If you cheat and don't get caught, you're a hero. If you cheat and get caught, you're a dope. Put me in the category where you think I belong.' "

Trace turned to look at Harlan. "So where do I belong?"

"You belong where you are right now—on top of the

heap," Harlan said. "With tonight's checkered, you're Midwestern points leader in Super Stocks."

Much later, in his cabin, Trace felt the big Blu hauler gear down from freeway speed, the Allison transmission braking them—*shoom*, and *shooom*, and *shoooooom*—as it downshifted. The rig rocked slightly as it slowed to a crawl. Still in his race clothes, he sat up in bed. He had sent Mel at least ten texts—with no reply. Each message was shorter than the last, until there were no more ways to say he was sorry.

He stood up and went to his porthole. Harlan was docking at the diesel pumps at the big Clearwater Travel Plaza, Freeway 94, near St. Cloud, Minnesota. They were headed to Minneapolis for a special appearance at the Mall of America, then on to Wisconsin for racing. This was a serious truck stop, with a long, tight row of eighteen-wheelers on the back side, their drivers catching some sleep, and a dozen pump lanes for "civilian" cars lit by harsh vapor lights. Trace had stopped here often with his parents on the way to Minneapolis and St. Paul—mainly because the place had a major bakery.

Remembering that he hadn't eaten since early afternoon, Trace rummaged through his clothes for his wallet. Below, Harlan clanked the nozzle into the mouth of the saddle tank. Trace headed down, then stepped outside into the cool night air. Smoky and Jimmy were already on

their way to the bakery. Smoky's motor home sat just
behind the big hauler, with Harlan on the back side of the
tractor, running the fuel. Trace paused, glanced around,
then stepped over to Smoky's rig. He tried the door. It was
open. With one more quick look around, he slipped inside.

The place smelled like tools. Like fuel and WD-40 and
GoJo hand cleaner and Little Trees air freshener. Jimmy's
bunk, with rumpled sleeping bag, was over the cab, and
Smoky's bedroom was in the rear. In between, covering
the little galley kitchen and all available counter and cush-
ion space, were voltmeters, ohmmeters, electrical probes,
remote-control devices, little boxes with joysticks that
looked homemade, several types of magnets small to large,
along with parts and pieces of cell phones. Those were all
gathered around several silvery Holley carburetors. Trace
picked up the nearest carb. It was way light in his hand—
he knew the weight of a Holley two-barrel—and he turned
it over. Parts of the underside were missing. He set it
down and examined another carburetor. This one weighed
right but had bright grinding and polishing marks on the
side. Holding it close to his eyes, he saw a nearly invisible
slot—with a tiny sliding window—no wider than a pencil
eraser. The alterations were machined as finely as an
expensive watch.

The door latch clicked behind him. Trace whirled.
Smoky stood there, silhouetted in the narrow doorway.

"It's way simpler than you think," he said. His face was
shadowy.

"I'm sorry," Trace began. He glanced around the trailer.

Smoky shrugged. "I'd do the same thing if I were you—snoop around, try to figure things out."

Trace looked again at the carburetor in his hand. He touched the altered spot. "It lets in more gas—I knew it," he said.

Smoky stepped forward and took the carburetor from Trace; he carefully set it back in its place. "No. These were all experiments that failed. Getting more gas through the carb and into the cylinders was the obvious choice. But the best engineering solution is always the simplest—and the least obvious."

"I don't get it," Trace said. "If it's not more gas—"

"Then what's the only other answer? Come on—you're a motor guy."

"More air," Trace said. "It's airflow!"

Smoky smiled his crooked smile. Jimmy arrived—and drew up in surprise to see Trace inside the motor home.

"I need to know how you do it," Trace said.

"Why?" Smoky asked.

"Because he's one of the good guys," Harlan said from behind Jimmy. There was sarcasm in his voice. "He's got the world by the tail, and he can't leave well enough alone."

"I can understand that," Smoky said. "I'd want to know, too."

"Well, I don't," Harlan said. "And neither does Jimmy. If we don't know, nobody can say we were lying."

Jimmy looked uncertainly at Smoky and Trace, then turned to follow his father into the cab.

"Come, I'll show you," Smoky said. "You deserve to know."

Trace followed him inside the hauler. The bright lights came on—Smoky flinched at the glare, then bent to the hood. Trace unpinned one side and Smoky the other. Carefully they hoisted away the bonnet.

"Take off the air-cleaner collar," Smoky said.

Trace obeyed.

"Now the air cleaner itself."

Trace spun off the wing nut from the vertical center pole, and lifted the air filter hoop. Beneath it was the platter-size round plate that the filter rested upon. In the center was the open throat of the carburetor. He leaned in to look at the carb.

"You missed it already," Smoky said.

Trace cocked his head one way, then the other.

"Just like the tech guys. They watch too many of those CSI shows. They want to do an autopsy, when the answer is way simpler."

Trace stepped back. "I still can't see how you're getting more airflow."

Smoky stepped up. With a small pliers, he unscrewed the vertical rod, threaded on top, that held in place the air-cleaner assembly. Every car had one. He tapped it on a roll cage pipe: *ting!* It rang bright and empty-sounding.

"It's hollow," Trace said.

Smoky handed it over.

Trace looked at its open end. "It's not a bolt, it's a tube."

"It's both," Smoky said.

Trace held its open end to his lips, and blew; the pipe whistled like a tiny piccolo.

"It puts more air right down into the carb," Smoky said. "Increases your cfm by about ten percent."

"That's why it always felt like I had more than a two-barrel carb."

"Not always," Smoky said.

"Just when you thought I needed it," Trace added.

"Which wasn't often." There was pride in Smoky's voice.

Trace examined the pipe once more—then held it close to the side of the Super Stock: it sucked against the tin with a sharp *clack!*

"Very good," Smoky said.

"It's magnetized," Trace said. "That, with the antennas, the satellite dish, the remote controls—somehow you made it open and close."

Smoky carefully retrieved his pipe. "A magician never gives away all his secrets," he said, and began to reassemble the air-cleaner parts.

Trace leaned against the car and let out a long breath. "So now what?"

"I guess that's up to you, kid," Smoky said as he worked.

"I can't drive if I know we're cheating."

"And I can't not do my job," Smoky said.

"Your job is to cheat?" Trace said.

"I don't call it that," Smoky said. "I make cars go fast—faster than other cars. So fast, nobody else can catch them. That's how stock car racing began, and that's how it still is. It's my job to give you the fastest car on the track, and it's the rules guys' job to catch me. I'm only doing what Laura Williams and the people above her hired me to do: 'Whatever it takes,' they said."

"What about Harlan and Jimmy?"

"They don't know what I do or how I do it. They're just country boys tryin' to keep racin' and make a living," Smoky said. "Down South it's tough if your family name ain't Allison or Petty."

Trace swallowed. He ran his hand along the smooth blue tin of the Super Stock.

Smoky looked sideways at Trace. "And don't fool yourself, kid," he said. "Racing is way bigger than any one driver. If you walk away, Laura will have another kid behind the wheel tomorrow."

"I don't want to walk away," Trace said. "But if we keep cheating, I'll never really know how good a driver I am."

"Well, get used to that, because I've always got more tricks up my sleeve. If I can get one of those other carburetors to work right—"

Harlan and Jimmy appeared in the doorway.

"Come on in," Smoky said. "We're about done here."

"Yes, we are," Trace said suddenly. He stiffened his spine.

Harlan and Jimmy looked at Trace uncertainly.

"I can't drive for you anymore," Trace said to them.

"What?" Harlan exclaimed.

"Not this way," Trace said.

"What way? We're winning!"

"I want to be *legal* and win."

Smoky shrugged, shook his head with a mixture of sadness and disgust, and left the trailer.

"What are we gonna do now, Pops?" Jimmy murmured. His face had turned pale and scared.

"Don't worry about that," Harlan replied, keeping his angry eyes on Trace. "One monkey don't stop the show."

Trace shrugged. "Well, I'm no longer the Team Blu monkey," he said. He turned, headed up to his cabin, and threw his stuff in his duffel bag. It was surprising how few things actually belonged to him.

When he came down, Harlan and Jimmy were still there, waiting. Jimmy looked away; Trace saw a glint of extra water in his eyes.

"That monkey crack," Harlan began. "That's not exactly what I meant."

Trace waited.

"I meant, Laura will have a new driver tomorrow," Harlan said. "Drivers are a dime a dozen, but good ones— like you—are hard to find."

Trace looked squarely at Harlan. "But with Smoky

building my engines, and you looking the other way, how would I ever know how good I am?"

A pause followed. Jimmy's eyes flickered back and forth between Harlan and Trace.

Harlan stiffened his back and put on his gruff face. "Okay, kid. I can sort of see what you're saying. And you're only eighteen. I've been there. So let's do this: why don't you go into the truck stop and cool off for a while? Get yourself a cup of coffee. Try to relax and think this through. Think about what you'd be throwing away."

"I could go with him," Jimmy said quickly.

"No," Harlan said sharply. "Trace has to do this on his own."

Jimmy's shoulders pulled in; he said nothing more.

"Okay, I will," Trace said. "I owe you that much."

"But we roll in fifteen minutes," Harlan said, looking at his watch. "You're either on board or you're not."

Trace swallowed, shouldered his duffel bag, and walked out. Across the empty, brightly lit lot, past the silent gas pumps. He checked the time on his phone.

Inside, he stepped up to the counter.

"What do you need?" asked a sleepy-looking older woman. Trace wondered more and more about people: what things—what decisions—in her life had brought her to this moment?

"Coffee."

"Dark roast, medium, or light?" she asked in automatic reply.

"Whatever. Medium, I guess."

Hot cardboard cup in hand, he went to the narrow side counter and sat on a stool. He took his time opening three creamers; each one made his black coffee a shade lighter. After he stirred the coffee, he pushed the little plastic cups into a triangle. Like a shell game—which one covers the pea? But tonight there was no pea.

He looked around the diner at the scattering of other late-night types, all alone, then checked the time again. He called Mel, but she didn't pick up; he didn't leave a message. He thought of calling his father, but didn't.

The coffee was horrible, and after a few sips he pushed it aside. He could see, through the front window glass, the big blue hauler, waiting beyond the far pumps. As the deadline approached—two minutes left—he carried his duffel bag to the front of the store. Near the door.

One minute.

Harlan revved the engine and brought up all the lights. It really was a beautiful rig.

"That your ride?" the guy at the till asked.

Trace swallowed. Ever so slowly, the Team Blu rig began to move. "No," Trace said. "It's not."

The long hauler eased away. At the stop sign, its brake lights came on; there was no oncoming traffic, but the brakes remained red—as if Harlan was waiting. Long seconds stretched toward half a minute—and then the tractor jerked forward sharply, pulling the trailer onto the highway. Its running lights streamed sideways as they headed away, and then gradually disappeared into the night.

Trace went back to the counter. He spent a long time texting Mel. He told her about April, and also about Sara Bishop. The truth of both was way less bad than Mel believed. He told her about leaving Team Blu—and that he was coming home. After that he called his father.

When he finally set down his phone, the coffee woman came by, this time pushing a broom. Her gaze fell to Trace's big duffel bag. "You got a ride somewhere?"

"Yes," Trace said. "I'm waiting for my father. He'll be here"—he checked his watch—"in a couple of hours. If that's all right."

"No problem, we're open all night," she said. Then she cocked her head to look at him again. "Your face seems familiar. I keep thinking I should know you."

"I don't think so," Trace said. "But maybe someday you will."

"And how would that be?" the woman said, mustering a small smile.

"I'm a race-car driver," Trace said.